Arising

two novellas and a play by

Lorne Shirinian

Also by Lorne Shirinian

Poetry
Manuscript: Tom Sturgess
Poems of Dispersion and Other Rites of Movement
Earthquake
Rough Landing
Rendering the Timeline

Fiction
The Key and Other Stories
Beginnings and Ends
History of Armenia and Other Fiction
Memory's Orphans
When Darkness Falls Upon Us Love
Hemorrhage
What Remains
Transformations: Selected Short Fiction, 1977-2005
Restlessness
Intimate Spaces
Like Standing on Shifting Sands
Simantov

Drama
Exile in the Cradle
This Dark Thing: Two One-Act Plays
Monumental

Life Writing
So Far from Home
Motion Sickness: a memoir

Literary and Cultural Criticism

Armenian-North American Literature, a Critical Introduction: Genocide, Diaspora and Symbols

The Republic of Armenia and the Rethinking of the Diaspora in Literature

The Impact of the Armenian Genocide: Eighty-Three Years of Survival and Memory in the Armenian Diaspora

Survivor Memoirs of the Armenian Genocide

Quest for Closure: The Armenian Genocide and the Search for Justice in Canada

Writing Memory: The Search for Home in Armenian Diaspora Literature as Cultural Practice

The Armenian Genocide: Resisting the Inertia of Indifference (co-written with Alan Whitehorn)

The Landscape of Memory: Perspectives on the Armenian Diaspora

Arising, two novellas and a play, First Canadian Edition, Blue Heron Press, 2023

© 2023 by Lorne Shirinian, 1945-

ISBN 978-0-920266-60-1

Blue Heron Press, 502 – 1135 Logan Avenue, Toronto, Ontario, Canada M4K 3Y2

Visit the following websites for a full list of Lorne Shirinian's books.

www.blueheronpress.ca

https://www.writersunion.ca/member/lorne-shirinian

Arising

For Noémi

Arising

Prologue

Some days, you wake thinking that it's going to be a normal morning, a slow build-up to the usual frustrations you can handle. Before long, signs appear that you will recognize too late that things are not right. It soon becomes clear that your day has placed you in a world that no longer recognizes you. You are surprised when you realize that everything is out to suppress you, deny your identity, your history, and your life. As the space around you shrinks, you can only rely on three friends, one of whom is a stranger. You find as Manuel Sweet does, in *It Never Ends* that the state apparatus driven by fear and fueled by incorrect information has decided to pursue you. Your late father, with whom you had argued for years, is the only one who can save you.

Jake Armen left his home in Toronto soon after his university studies to live and write in Paris. Fifty years later, he returns home with little to show for his dream and rents a room in a B & B very near where he grew up. He soon discovers that the owner is a person he went through public and high school with. She is a retired crime reporter for a well-known city newspaper. As they reminisce, they discover that they both have been haunted by an event that happened to them when they were in grade two, the drowning of one of their classmates. Both have felt that there was more to the death of their friend and that no one offered an explanation as to why the young boy died. That shared history continues to disturb them and motivates them to study the case. Like ripples spreading out from their dead friend's body lying in the Don River, Jake's return turns on many moments from his past that he has never wished to confront, things that have been *Held Under*.

In *Port Cities*, the four main characters from the two novellas now find themselves out of a story. They have been asked to come to an island in the eastern Mediterranean where the writer has told them he will show up to discuss a new tale and a chance to work again. While they wait and hope, they drink wine, discuss, argue and plan. Despite his promises, the writer does not show up. Deeply disappointed by their creator, the four characters decide to leave the island and to leave the writer to his own devices.

The two novellas and the one-act play in this collection are a study of change over time and the way individuals react to the forces required to deal with transformations, with history.

L S

Toronto, February 23, 2023

It Never Ends

Life can only be understood backwards, but it must be lived forwards.

Soren Kierkegaard

1

"Something's wrong. I know it." Manuel Sweet turned over and tried to sleep, but the feeling had disturbed him for the past few weeks and had grown stronger. Someone had been following him. He was certain of it. There were new cars parked at night on the street near his home. Just last night, in the yellow light of the streetlamp, he could see the driver, wearing headphones, sitting, listening and making notes. During the day when he was out, he was sure he recognized the same faces following him. It wasn't a coincidence. To be sure, he walked different routes, but they were still there, sometimes behind him or up ahead across the street. That he was sure of. But why? He rolled over to his right side and stared at the half bookshelf in the bedroom. Who could they be? His eyes became heavy, and the books became a blur. The questions became thicker. Why is someone after me? The night had become black. It had become difficult to think. How can I discover who? His last thought that night was Aaron. Call Aaron.

When Manuel Sweet entered university in 1973, his generation had already been rebelling against everything for years. If you couldn't find a cause, you made one up, and before long, many would join. Signs would be held high angrily proclaiming the righteousness of the issue. Later, those who were digitally literate developed the ability to bypass fences and sentinels, creating new ways in the arts and in politics, forcing the old guard to rethink their positions. In the end, the gatekeepers knew they had to maintain what they knew was right, even as the walls had already been breached. The revolution was moving rapidly. In the ensuing havoc, many became trapped in the chaos and couldn't free themselves from the nets.

For others, history and identity became their cause. In part, it was the strength of multicultural, cosmopolitan societies. The new engulfed the old, creating chasms among family members who could not understand what the world they had known had been turned into. It was new, full of energy and aggressively meaningful. Literature, art, theatre, and cinema spoke to people in a different way. Life for youth was playful and exciting. Everything was interchangeable. Everything was expendable and replaceable because everything was consumable and disposable.

The past needed to be repaired. There had to be justice before one could join the dance. Many became committed to healing the past that always seemed to be there, bruised, bloodied, and bandaged, limping along, imploring its adherents to look backwards and to remember. Manuel's father Martiros was one who could not forget the past. When he was a five-year old boy, he had lost everything. His family had been driven into exile, force marched into the harsh desert of south-western Syria known as Der es-Zor. He never knew if his mother and father had actually survived the deportation, which was nothing more than a passage to mass slaughter or if they had arrived at the final desert destination where there was no food, water, or any provisions for them. Either way, for the Ottoman Turks, death was the desired outcome. As he grew into a young man, Martiros gave his life to the study of the Armenian

Genocide and had hoped that Manuel would follow in his footsteps. The denial the perpetrators had spread since 1915 needed to be combated. The victims and people of good conscience needed to have the truth known. This had become his life's work. It had pained him grievously that Manuel had chosen another path for his life's work.

Now in the spring of 2022 at the age of sixty-seven, Manuel was an ex-professor of literature and a full-time writer of many novels, poems and plays only seven of which had actually made it onto the shelves of the bookstores in his city and around the world. He still lived alone in his parents' house where he was working on a new novel that likely would have a very short print run; that is, if he ever finished and had it published. "I'm running out of time," he often would say out loud as he searched for a book in his large library that would help advance his story. Lately, something had disturbed his progress. It was worse than a grain of sand under his eyelid. He had the distinct impression that someone was after him. With each passing day, it became clearer that what was left of his future was in jeopardy. He worried that he would succumb to the forces against him and disappear as did so many of his grandparents' generation. His father Martiros had wanted him to focus on their history. This was always a source of friction between them. Although Manuel respected the weight of his father's opinion, he navigated his own way through this turmoil, which at times brought him close to floundering.

2

Manuel's mother Marie had passed in 1970 at the age of fifty-five after a long illness. He could still hear her voice in the morning calling him from the kitchen when he woke, "Get dressed and come down, Manuel. Breakfast is ready. You'll be late for classes." There was always tenderness in the way she had raised him. His father, who had driven him to excel in everything he did, had passed away twenty-two years later in 1992. What had once been a close-knit family had now been reduced to him, their son Manuel, and he didn't feel close to anyone or anything.

His father's memories of surviving genocide in 1915 had remained the centre of his life and the focus of his research and writing; in the end, they were left silent in archive boxes. His father had told Manuel, "When I go, you will be the guardian of my memories. I am bequeathing to you these boxes of my essays and memoirs, and my library." He stretched his right arm out across the many bookshelves. "I have spent most of my life writing

and collecting it. It will be up to you to carry on."
He hugged his son. "It is a burden I am placing on
you. I was born into it and have lived with the
curse all my life. I wanted to take it with me to my
grave, but there is more that needs to be said. I
know you will redeem us." Three weeks later on
November 15, 1992, at the age of eighty-two, his
father passed away, and the full weight of what he
had asked had now fallen upon Manuel.

Manuel had studied literature at City
University. He was a gifted student and completed
his Honour BA and MA in French studies then
enrolled in the doctoral program in Comparative
Literature where he completed the course work,
supplementary examinations, and his doctoral
thesis on the literature of genocide in three years.
He received his PhD in 1986. Even before
graduation, he had been offered teaching positions
at universities in Canada and the U. S. but refused
to leave the city. He wanted to be near his father
to look after him especially after watching his
mother slowly succumb to her illness. City
University had offered him sessional work that

finally led to a tenured position in the Department of Comparative Literature in 1986. When he and his father argued about what he should be writing, he told him that his teaching and research were keeping him from doing what his father had wanted him to do. "I'm busy with my career, Papa." His father often chided him, "My past is also your past, my son. Attend to it."

After his father's funeral, Manuel went back to his parents' home and stood in his father's library which now had become his. He realized that his father's story and all his work would soon remain only on library shelves or disappear into the deep sinkhole of history, gone forever. He took out the many archive boxes that contained all of his father's writing and published work and sat on a chair and began reading them again. As he went through folder after folder, he knew he would have to write the story of how his father lived with the planned destruction of his people and their culture. He was called upon to honour his father and mother and turn their lives into a legacy. "Read my work as documents of personal and family responsibility," his father had told him. "Perhaps with the passage of time, you will find your place in the world without the oppressive weight of our past. I have never been able to."

He picked out a folder dated May 1942 and opened it to find a memoir of an early moment during the genocide when as a young boy of five in 1915, his father was first confronted with the full horror of the massacres.

When the smoke began to clear and the rifle shots and the screaming stopped, I raised my head and crawled out of the small cave in the woods behind our home that had become my secret hiding place. In the intense stillness, bodies had been left as a warning to others. I recognized some of them left in front of their homes, some face down in the dirt; others I saw on their backs their startled eyes bereft of hope in the final moments of their agony. I can still hear them imploring. 'Please! Have mercy! O, God!' Blood and shit stained the earth.

Where does one go when there is no safe place left? When house, home, and family have been destroyed? All I could do was run. I followed creeks, streams, and rivers, climbed hills and crossed plains, keeping low, disappearing. I took food from orchards and fields. When I heard human voices, I ran in the other direction. As the world collapsed in on me, it also opened out. I learned not to trust anyone, not to believe in anything. Only the freedom to take the next step mattered.

His father had written on a separate sheet of paper left in the folder. "To be added for the revised version." On it, he had noted events of the Holocaust that had taken place twenty-seven years later in May 1942, when he had written this memoir.

May 1942 - SS officials selected the first group of victims for gassing at Auschwitz-Birkenau. Prisoners who were deemed weak, sick, and unfit were taken to a bunker where they were gassed with Zyklon B gas. Between May

1940 and January 1945, more than one million people were killed at this camp.

May 27, 1942 - In occupied Belgium, German authorities issued a decree requiring all Jews to wear the yellow star.

May 29, 1942 - German authorities required all Jews residing in France to wear the yellow Star on their outer clothing, effective June 7.

When he was a young teenager, Manuel had asked his father about his youth. "What was it like then, Papa? You never told me. How did you get to be here, meet mama, and find work?"

"There are good people in this world," he said. "A few found me after the massacres. They believed that putting me in an orphanage with other unfortunate young ones was a solution. They made us go to school to learn language and history. I refused to go to church. How could anyone after all that? Then one day a chance to leave presented itself, and I took it, and after a long voyage on a ship with others across the Mediterranean and over the Atlantic, I landed here. When I arrived, I was told, 'You'll have a new chance.' I learned that life always seems to have hidden tricks to play on us. I naïvely thought that those who have lost all, might be spared to try again in another place. It's never that simple."

Manuel sat rapt as his father spoke of his life. "I won't say things were just as bad here. I had a sense that a degree of hope might be warranted. In time, years in fact, I found your mother, and we married. Her family had survived and ended up in France. We both worked hard to build a future. You came into our lives. Yet, I could never free myself from the images of our neighbours lying murdered near their homes and everything else I had seen on the roads where people had been massacred. Can you imagine how hard it was for me to believe that life made sense? Work hard. Pay your bills. All will be good. How? For whom?"

When Manuel visited his father for the last time in the hospital, he held him gently. He was so frail, his body almost weightless. He finally felt free to let his guard down. Manuel cried as he said his goodbyes. "It's an odd journey," his father whispered, as his last breaths were taken with increasing difficulty. "Having you and your mother...." His voice became muffled then disappeared. There was more he wanted to say but the effort was too much. In the end, there is always silence.

Manuel buried his father next to his mother and returned to his routine at the university. As the new millennium approached, he began to get restless and paid less attention to his research and teaching. At the end of the semester, he resigned from his position at the university, emptied his apartment, and moved back into his parents' home which he had maintained. When Professor Baruch Curiel, his mentor at the university, had learned of this, he called him to come to his office. "You're only at the beginning of an important career, Manuel. Think carefully about this."

"I will still be involved," Baruch, "just not academically. There are things I need to do at this time."

"Are you looking for closure?"

"I don't think that's possible."

"In my experience, there rarely is," he said. He went back to his desk and picked up a folder.

"Manuel, your father gave me a text he had written in 1985. It's important. When I wrote to him, he asked me to keep it for him, but I think he meant for me to keep it for you. I don't know how long I'll be here," he said. "When I pass, who knows what the administration will do with my effects? I have no family to leave my things to. You should have it."

Manuel had made plans to go to Paris and work his way east to the small remnant of land that had become the republic of his father's nation. It was his idea of a pilgrimage his father would have suggested. His flight to Paris was scheduled to depart at seven on a Tuesday evening. He threw his knapsack over his shoulders and pulled a small suitcase along behind him. He had what he needed and walked over to Yorkville where he had lunch then took an airport bus to Pearson International where he waited in the departure lounge in silence and read. He wasn't sure what to hope for. He knew he just needed to keep moving.

As the clock began to approach flight time, Manuel began to feel an uncomfortable twinge in his stomach. He should have boarded by now, yet there was no one behind the desk at the gate. Equally strange, he was still the only passenger in the lounge waiting to fly to Paris.

He slipped on his backpack and grabbed the handle of his suitcase and went out into the main hall which had become a chaos of people maneuvering around each other and through long lines of anxious passengers. Feeling slightly panicky, he returned to the counter where he had checked in almost two hours earlier and showed his ticket. "Oh, there's no flight there today," the attendant said and looked at him with a curious smile. "So why wasn't I told anything when I checked in here and showed one of your colleagues my ticket?" She shook her head. "Don't know. I wasn't here. Were there others waiting in the departure lounge?"

"No, I was the only one."

"Wasn't that a clue that something was off?"

"I can see that now," he said. "This conversation is another sign that something isn't right. When is the next flight to my destination?"

"Tomorrow at the same time, seven pm. I can exchange your ticket for that flight."

He handed her his ticket and watched her input his information into their computer system for what seemed like a longer time than necessary.

"There you are. You're all set for tomorrow at the same time. I've given you the same seat," she said cheerfully. "Arrive early to avoid complications due to the rush at that time."

He nodded to her and turned around and faced the long line of passengers waiting to check in. He wanted to yell that it's all a joke. There are no flights.

Manuel wasn't going to wait at the airport for twenty-four hours. He took a bus back into the city. When it let him off at the imperious Royal York Hotel, he instinctively felt that he shouldn't return to his home. Something felt off. It struck him that now he had nowhere to go. He felt like a stranger, an alien arriving for the first time in a strange city. He had no choice but to find a hotel.

In front of him stood the imposing façade of the Royal York Hotel. He knew that if he weren't careful, he would burn through his savings quickly, but what could he do in these circumstances? Alone, tired, and hungry, he was beginning to feel the anxiety a tourist feels when arriving for the first time in a new city. He entered with trepidation and checked in.

Later that evening after a decent dinner followed by two cups of espresso, he returned to his room and watched news reports. There were vague accounts of several disturbances at airports throughout Europe. At the same time, waves of immigrants had tried to land on an island near Sicily. Ten from one boat had drowned in the attempt. They were all desperate to get into Europe despite not having any documents. He wondered whether his flight cancellation could have been a result of these. Unable to deal with the stress of the day that should have seen him high in the sky on the way to Paris, he let it all go and fell into a troubled sleep in a room with coats of arms on every wall, staring down at him.

In the morning after a café Americano and a croissant with butter and apricot jam in the Sovereign Lounge, he decided to call the airline company at the airport to verify the status of his flight. A distant, crackling voice responded, "One moment, please, I'll check." After an inordinately long time, a man with an aggressively dry voice spoke. "Your flight YYX-CDN is leaving at seven this evening; however, your name is not on the passenger list."

"But…but…." He tried to break in as his anger was rising. "I have a ticket," he told him. Manuel gave him the number and the information on the receipt.

"Yes, well," he said, "the flight will be leaving, but you will not be on it."

"Why not? What's going on?"

"*Raison d'état*. That's all I know. This came directly from the French Embassy. You will not be allowed on this flight or any flight. I can't do anything for you. *Au revoir*."

Manuel wondered what he could do, and more pressingly, where he could go. He would have to stay another night in the hotel until he got this straightened out. He knew that *raison d'état* is the principle that a state can give itself the right to violate its own norms in the interest of a higher interest such as the protection of the state. What could that be in my case, he wondered? He was a writer with a few books to his credit. I have opinions. Sometimes I express them forcefully. Surely, that couldn't be it.

Back in his expensive room at the hotel, he decided to call the French embassy in Ottawa. After another long wait, he was told that a European security agency had put him on a watch status. "If you travel to France, you will be arrested. That's all the information we have."

"But I've done nothing," he protested. "What is the problem?"

"You must have done something, monsieur."

"How can I find out? Whom can I call?"

"I don't know, but if I were you, I would not go to the airport this evening. Let me offer you another piece of advice. He whispered into the receiver, "Leave the hotel. *Au revoir.*"

Something was not right. He decided to take the advice the man at the embassy had given him and checked out. On his way out, the attendant to whom he had spoken earlier recognized him. "No luck then, sir?"

Manuel replied, "I didn't realize that getting to Paris was so difficult."

"It seems you are a special case. Thank you for staying with us."

Manuel turned to thank her and saw that she was speaking on the phone. He caught the end of her conversation, "He's on his way out now." She couldn't have meant me, he thought. That would be crazy. He looked around the lobby and walked slowly towards the main doors and exited onto Front Street, where he hailed a cab.

3

He didn't want to admit it, but he felt a trap was enclosing around him. His plan after leaving the country was to spend a few days in Paris then take the TGV train to Marseilles then a coastal train along the Riviera, hopping off and on at various towns to relax in the sun and taste the local dishes. Eventually, he would have ended up in Florence. Then, after a few days in the city, he would have travelled down the east coast to Brindisi and would have taken a ferry to Corfu where the real purpose of his trip would have begun, visiting the orphanage on the island where in 1922 his father was placed with other homeless Armenians after the Genocide to escape the dangers of the Turkish War for Independence. His father had spent two years in Corfu under the auspices of the Lord Mayor's Fund of London. At the orphanage, he was chosen to be taken to a new orphanage this time far away in Canada, to the Farm Home for Armenian Orphans in Georgetown, Ontario, where, in 1924, he was given a new life in exchange for the one that the

Ottomans had destroyed. That was the beginning of his father's life in the New World.

From Corfu, Manuel had planned to travel to Athens. He had rejected the idea of going to his father's village, Houtbelank, which was part of the town of Geyve in Sakarya province in Turkey even though he would have been relatively close. What was there for him, but unanswerable questions and painful memories passed down? There was nothing to discover. Lost families were gone forever; the destruction and pain continue.

The final leg would have taken him to Yerevan, Armenia, where he knew no one. No doubt he would have been amazed and proud that the people survived and thrived despite continuing hardships. He would have had to face the question whether he was a long-lost brother or just a stranger passing through. The country and its people suffered a genocide from 1915 to 1918 and its ongoing after-effects, Soviet oppression for almost seventy years, and two brutal wars with Azerbaijan, the first from 1988 to 1994 to establish the Armenian enclave of Nagorno-Karabakh, called Artsakh in Armenian. The second took place in 2020-2021, during which Armenia suffered many casualties as the Azeris had been well supplied with sophisticated weapons which they paid for with oil money. His father's country always seemed to be on the brink of financial collapse or being invaded and rendered a vassal state, once again a protectorate of Russia. Reduced in space despite independence in 1991, Armenia was on the verge of being cancelled.

It was clear that he wasn't going anywhere. Going south to America didn't seem like a good idea given the watch report on him. Then a break. Aaron, his good friend from his past, called to reply to the message Manuel had left him. They had been neighbours and had grown up together in East York, played on the same sports teams and had gone through school and university together. With time, they had grown apart as their professional lives demanded their attention. Aaron had gone into law, and Manuel into academia, literature, writing and books. "Come over. It's been a long time. We need to catch up."

They hugged and went over old times in the living room sharing a bottle of Shiraz. Aaron ordered food in and an hour later they finished off the last drops of another bottle. Aaron had done well for himself. His new house had been designed by Stein & Azulay, a well-known company in the city. The clean lines and original artwork on white walls gave a sense of space that was comforting to Manuel. After, they went for a walk in the neighbourhood. It was late spring, and the days were getting longer though the nights were still cool. They reminisced about the past and speculated about their futures. "I'm thinking of retiring," Aaron said. "I've been doing this for a long time. I'm ready to step back and relax, try something different. How about you?"

"I retired from the university some time ago. In or out, it's all the same, books and writing. There's nothing else I really want to do."

"We did all right. In some way, we tried to make a difference."

It wasn't Manuel's intention to tell Aaron about his problem right away, but when Aaron said, "We did all right," the moment presented itself. He explained that a European security agency was looking for him. "I don't know why," he said. "My bank accounts are frozen. I had hoped to fly to Paris last night, but I've been warned that it's not safe to board an airplane. No one will tell me anything other than that there is a security watch on me."

"Can you think of anything you might have done? You were heavily into fighting genocide denial."

"I was part of legitimate protests. I spoke out, published articles. That's all."

"You know that the political climate has changed considerably since those days. Commerce is king. People are not interested in hearing about events that took place far away over a hundred years ago."

"I was doing it for my parents. You know my family history. My grandparents, aunts and uncles were killed for being Armenian."

They went to the beige sofa sitting on the dark-stained, wide oak planks in the living room and continued. "Listen, this is a coincidence; I'm leaving for a human rights conference in Paris tomorrow night. I'll make some calls to see if I can discover anything." Aaron stopped and looked at him. "Tell me you haven't been mixed up in anything that could have brought this down on you."

"This sounds like a cross examination. I have not done anything that could have caused my life to be cancelled. I've been committed to the cause, not stupid."

They sat back and continued reminiscing about their youth and the people they knew who had come and gone, and the fun times they had together. "Do you remember," Manuel asked, "when our hockey coach came to pick us up for a seven-a.m. game? We had our equipment bags and sticks with us and hid in the valley.

"He was so angry when he left without us. He needed us and couldn't bench us for the next game."

"We were always headstrong and unpredictable, Aaron. Tell me, has it all turned out the way you thought it would?"

"For the most part, yes. As you can see, I've done well. I don't have much of a life apart from my law practice. We're the same, I think. We're doing what we love."

"Yes. I have to say that I suspected it would come to this after years of telling the world about the Genocide. I had hoped it would have been different. Their tactic is still to deny it all, accuse the victims, and finally, silence the messenger."

The black night turned pale purple until the arc of the sun brightened the horizon. Aaron got up and stretched. "You can stay here for as long as you need to. Tomorrow is a busy day. I have to finish work at my office then prepare for the conference. I'll leave the key and the entry code on the kitchen counter along with a letter letting anyone know that you have my permission to stay here. I'll tell my secretary as well. Do you have money?"

"I have enough for now, thanks."

"I'll be gone by 8:30. I'll call you during the day. When you go out, be mindful. Check to see if there is anyone or a car parked nearby. Be cautious. Good night."

"You mean good morning."

He was fatigued by everything that had taken place. As Manuel put his head down on the pillow, he thought that sometimes, the past can be a mercy.

4

On the second day after Aaron's departure, Manuel received a short email from him. "Made some preliminary inquiries. Nothing. I'll stay on it. Hope you're well. You should get out. Clear your mind. More later. Best."

Manuel took his advice and stood in front of the house. The weather had begun to transition from late spring to early summer. The air was sweet with hints of warmth. He looked up and down the street. Nothing stood out except for a black Ford sedan facing south. He began to walk towards it hugging the curb. It was empty. Inside he saw that it was a basic model, perhaps the kind a government would buy when it ordered a fleet for its agents. Manuel wrote down the number of the license plate.

Sometime later as he approached Avenue Road and Bloor, he began to wonder whether he was becoming paranoid. Maybe that's what they expected. He might laugh it off and let his guard down. He would have plenty of time to analyze his error in a small cell. He kept on reminding himself not to stand out. Be vigilant. Aware. Mindful.

Next to the Church of the Redeemer on the northeast corner, there was a café nested in the little plaza. He noticed there were two doors allowing a quick exit out of one if he sensed danger. He shook his head as he realized that this is what his life had come to in his sixty-seventh year.

He ordered an espresso and sat at a corner table. He took out his notebook and unscrewed the cap of his fountain pen. An idea for a new play had come to him a few days earlier. The questions he needed to ask himself suddenly seemed more pertinent today. What does the hero want to accomplish? What is his goal? What compels him? Freedom and safety, of course. Who else will suffer if he doesn't achieve his goal? Must create empathy. The audience has to care about him. Then he thought about the antagonist who has the opposite goal. He must be ruthlessly committed to achieving his aim. There can be only one winner. What happens if the hero fails? The stakes must be high. The more he thought about it, the more he needed to write this play even though at this moment it was manifestly depressing. He finished his espresso and looked around. A tall man in a light blue suit came in and ordered. He looked around at the customers. Manuel felt uncomfortable as he felt he zeroed in on him. He quickly and quietly left by the door at his end of the café. Outside, he stood behind an ornamental tree and watched the man in the suit exit holding his coffee. He nodded to a friend who was waiting for him outside. His partner pointed in Manuel's direction. It was time to leave.

5

In an essay Manuel's father had penned in his late thirties, he had detailed how the men protecting the villages and towns in 1915 always had the element of surprise as they knew the terrain, the roads, and paths, the best vantage points. The troops from the metropole often were made up of raw recruits sent out to get their first taste of blood in their genocidal plan. Their bravado encouraged by the corporals and sergeants rarely masked the fear beating in their hearts. "We fought and they died. We fought and we died. In the end, we held our lines because there was nowhere else go. It was either hold or disappear." Manuel walked the streets wondering if he should return and clear out his things from Aaron's house. Stealth and constant movement had now become his watchwords. Would his father have considered this a retreat?

He took a long circuitous route back to Aaron's place and stood in the shadow of an old elm tree across the road. The black Ford sedan was still parked down the road. It appeared that it had been moved closer to Aaron's house. When a station wagon pulled into a driveway several homes away, he used this as a distraction to enter quickly and quietly. He unplugged his laptop and packed his knapsack and then drank some orange juice for energy. He exited through the back door and hopped a few fences and came out five streets further west.

After an hour of walking backstreets and alleys, he had to decide. Should he try for a train at Union Station on Front Street and head for Montréal or take a bus north, maybe to Collingwood where he could disappear among groups of tourists visiting the Blue Mountains? No one would think of looking for him up there. However, he calculated that his escape routes were limited as he didn't drive and didn't know the area that far north of the city. Montréal looked like the better option.

He walked some more to clear his head and found himself in Kensington Market in front of Rosie's Bakery Café. The pastries in the window were too much to argue with. He went in and ordered and sat at one of the three unoccupied tables. The crunch of the flaky pastry released a burst of the apricot filling that flooded his senses. For a Proustian moment, he went blind to what was happening around him; the anxiety that now ruled his life prevented a delightful journey back to a special moment in his mother's kitchen. He was floating on the taste and texture as his heart was racing. He exhaled and came back to reality and sipped the dark espresso. It was a momentary escape. When he realized that he was scanning the sidewalk inadvertently, he knew he was still a prisoner of the plan to take him in.

Back out on the street, he breathed in the air and put on sunglasses. It was a glorious day, and he was on the run. When he got to Spadina Avenue, his phone buzzed. Aaron had sent him a text message. "Can't find anything that concerns you. Are you sure about this? Even contacted Interpol. They say they aren't looking for you. Is there some other group after you? Will call later. Suggest you go back to my place and relax. If anything happens, call me."

He made his way back to Aaron's place. He was still anxious, but no matter how hard he tried, he couldn't rid himself of this sense of guilt, that he had done something wrong. He needed to write, to explore his situation. He turned on his laptop and plugged in his external two-terabyte solid-state drive on which he kept all his files and research as well as many of his father's essays and memoirs which he had written throughout his life. Sometimes his father's essays were published; just as often they were not. No matter, for he kept everything in folders which along with the texts also contained notes explaining the reasons why he wrote the particular piece. Many essays were academic in nature and contained endnotes and a bibliography. This was the academic side of his father. Manuel always preferred his father's memoirs in which he gave information that he wanted to have as his son, as part of his family history. It was in his memoirs that his inner life shone and spoke to him. Manuel began by going over some of these works.

The first one he read was titled, "Memory, Caring and Morality," in which he asked, "What should we remember, and what should we forget?" He continued by defining the agency by which this process occurs, the moral witness, one who has experienced the suffering perpetrated by an evil regime. "The moral witness has not only observed but has also suffered, was at personal risk." His father believed that writing his memoirs had a moral purpose, a belief in the future. He recorded one of the human earthquakes of history that began in 1915 and continued beyond, the aftershocks of which are still felt deeply in communities today. He wrote what it was like to be in such a rupture. He had lost everything, family, and home, and like others of his nation was persecuted and hunted to death. Yet despite all the suffering, he was able to write lovingly of meeting Manuel's mother and bringing his son into the world he knew only too well could be a dangerous place. He worked at all sorts of jobs and managed to achieve his dream of getting a university education. It was at the City University where he met Professor Baruch Curiel, who had recognized that as a mature man, he had possessed a remarkable sensitivity and talent and worked with him to develop his knowledge and talent as a writer. Without this chance meeting, his life as well as his son's would not have been the same. *Ton père était sincère et authentique*, Baruch Curiel had told him the last time they had spoken. *C'est une chose rare de nos jours.*

At the end of his father's text, he had written, "I cannot forgive because it leads to forgetting. I cannot do this especially because the perpetrators continue to deny their injury to us even to the point of blaming us for their cruelty. This has meant for us that our identity, who we are, in large part, depends on us not forgetting the terrible things that happened to us. Thus, we must live with the pain. But for how long?"

6

The unprovoked aggression and willful destruction of civilians by the Russians are impossible to turn away from. The constant newsfeeds and reports from the field are heartbreaking, making everyone angry and depressed. Make it stop! People are shouting for revenge.

It's day seventeen of Putin's war on Ukraine. Mariupol is under continuous bombardment. People have no food, water, or medicine. To the northwest, Russian forces have now begun to encircle Kyiv, bombing the city indiscriminately. The west is supplying lethal weapons to the resolute defenders and many European countries continue to take in over two and a half million refugees. Hearing this, Manuel drove the pencil into a page of his notebook and wrote, Death to all tyrants. He remembered seeing a video taken of the final moments of the Romanian dictator, Nicolae Ceaușescu, and his wife Elena standing against a wall pleading for their lives moments before being shot. Two people who controlled the destiny of so many of their countrymen. A fitting end, but it doesn't seem enough for all the misery they caused. Will Putin face the same end?

After reading and listening to the gloomy news, Manuel decided to take Aaron's advice and go out. "It might be all in your mind," he had told him. Maybe, he's right, Manuel thought. He had asked Aaron to continue with his inquiries, and to let him know immediately if he finds even a hint of something.

"I promise," he had told him. "Get on with your life but remain cautious, Manny."

"Easy to say." His chest tightened. "I can't travel outside of the county, and my bank cards have been revoked. This isn't normal, Aaron. Somebody or something is after me. That's real."

Manuel stepped out onto the front porch and looked around. There were no cars parked on the street near Aaron's house. He followed the flight of a bird as it flew over the house and saw what looked like the end of a wire hanging from one of the eaves. He hadn't noticed it there yesterday.

Had the wind-blown it up there? Was it only a random small piece, or was it part of an antenna that was picking up voices inside? He went back inside and turned up the radio then collected his things and hit the streets, keeping an eye out for anything unusual. In the city, that would be just about everything.

Manuel took the subway then a streetcar to the Beach. He got off at Woodbine Avenue and walked along Queen Street East then went south on Waverly to the waterfront park. It was a lovely day; the sun was still high in the sky. The boardwalk was full of groups of young mothers pushing their baby strollers. At a café, he bought an espresso and walked a little until he found an empty bench under the shade of a tall maple tree. He sat and took in a deep breath and looked around. He wondered, what if two guys wearing dark sports jackets and blue ties on white shirts came up from behind and sat on each side of me and said, "Don't make any trouble. Get up and come with us." He looked around. It could happen, he thought. Lying on her back on a white blanket fifteen yards away was a young woman wearing yellow shorts and a blue tee-shirt, talking on her phone. He tried to tune in and thought he heard *We've got him.* He looked around. There was nobody nearby. He heard her say *Okay see you at 5:30.* He looked around again. It was a perfectly normal day at the beach. Small waves lapped the shore. White clouds blown by unseen winds scudded in the blue sky. Everyone was relaxing. He closed his eyes and asked, "What the hell is happening to me?" He breathed the fresh air and watched life happening. He couldn't have moved even if he had wanted to. It was a perfect moment.

He had fallen asleep for a while and woke with a start. The remains of his espresso had gone cold and bitter. He chided himself for not remaining alert. He turned on his laptop and through his still-foggy eyes searched through the list of his father's memoirs. Among all the files was a short one he hadn't read before. "The Wound That Never Heals." There was a footnote that appeared after the title. He looked at the bottom of the page.

"This is for my son Manuel, the first of our family born in the diaspora. He turned six today."

The first line read, "When they've forced you out and away from your home, you have to return with a gun." This was written in 1961. The country and its long history had been swallowed by an ideological machine in 1915 that chewed everything, digested all with its angry and pitiless juices and dropped its manure over everything so that generations would forever be tainted with its foul odor. He could hear his father's voice, "You have to return with a gun." All his life he wanted to reclaim the nation from those who had destroyed it then watched it destroyed again by its *saviors*. The individual and the nation. The anger had festered in him for most of his life. He turned to writing early to sharpen his thinking and his direct style. He spoke passionately when invited to conferences. A few years after Manuel had completed graduate school, he remembered his father standing before a large audience making the whole genocide understandable by focusing on his family who had remained only as a distant memory. No photos existed of any of them. All were killed; all was destroyed. Today, apart from him and his memoirs, no one knew they even existed. When he stood at a lectern before delivering a speech, he always said, "This is dedicated to my family" and said their names out loud. "All were killed, not for anything they had done, but for who they were and the difference they represented."

The starving Armenians known to all at the end of the World War I were still starving for recognition and justice today. Growing up, how could Manuel not have been imbued with his father's ideas and ideals? He too began writing and speaking out, participating in protest marches, doing what he could to bring what had occurred so many years ago back into public attention. However, Manuel soon learned that people tired of the aggressive nature of such action and turned to writing poetry, fiction and drama that dealt with the disinherited and forgotten. He became more introspective. It didn't take long to discover that the gatekeepers, literary critics, and publishers in this country, were timorous. Their bottom line loomed large. Their vision and historical knowledge were all too often limited, and they were easily distracted by small events. He broke away from the cultural machine and founded his own publishing house and began printing his own literary works that focused on the ongoing effects of the damages of history and genocide, how individuals and families continue to live with painful consequences. Sometimes, he knew, they are hidden or masked; often they are felt but ignored. The damage still exists even though it is unacknowledged. He knew many of his father's friends, also survivors, and their offspring who had lived with the aftermath of the Genocide. Some had engaged. Most sought to build a new life. None, however, forgot. They had buried it deep and lived with it.

Try as he did, the gatekeepers controlled the pathways, entrances, and gears of the machine. His books didn't often make it onto the shelves of bookstores. Interviews were rare. Rarer still were intelligent critical reviews in the major literary journals or on national radio programs. He kept hearing his father, *You have to return with a gun.*

7

Today the Russians are bombing closer to the Western border of Ukraine, closer to NATO countries. Putin continues to obliterate villages, towns and cities and all living things in his way to achieve his goal, his Putin the Great fantasy. Factory workers were forced to attend a rally in Moscow to celebrate the annexation of Crimea that took place in 2014. Putin stood on the stage in front of the flag-waving stooges daring to quote the Bible and lying about the government and people of Ukraine. He appeared to weigh four hundred pounds as the bullet-proof protection he wore made him look like Bip, the Michelin tire logo. The lies and the spectacle were grotesque. How many of those cheering actually believed it? In Russia, where truth is a rare commodity, perhaps many did, particularly those who grew up in the Soviet period and longed for the good-old days of fear, order, and oppression that Putin loves so much.

Sickened, Manuel needed to walk the streets of his city. He was almost out of cash and took a chance by going to the nearest branch of his bank. He didn't trust the pitiless logic of the algorithms of the bank-machine and chose to stand in line to see a teller. He took out his only remaining bank card and placed it before her. She swiped it and looked at the screen. She was motionless as she contemplated his request. Her eyes shifted over to him. "There's a problem." A tense moment passed. "Oh?" he offered. She moved closer to the window between them. Whispering so that only he could hear her, she said, "I'm supposed to hold your card. You aren't allowed to withdraw anything from your account."

"But how can I live?"

"I'm sorry."

"Can I not take anything from my account?"

"No, the system won't allow it. Is there another way?"

He spoke softly. "I have an account for my publishing house." He gave her the name and number. "I don't have a card for this account. Can

I make a withdrawal from it? Perhaps the system hasn't blocked this one."

She keyed in the information. This old account in which there was almost a thousand dollars to print his next book hadn't been sanctioned. "I'll take it all except for twenty dollars to keep the account open." He called it an act of optimism.

The teller's money drawer opened with a tight metallic sound from which she counted out the bills then placed them in two large envelopes. She sealed them and slid them through the small window. Manuel bent like a supplicant receiving the holy wafer. This host is the body of the bank. When you buy a drink with this money, it will be the blood of our bank from which your life may be saved. The young Asian woman touched his fingers as she put the lucre in his hands and smiled and mouthed, good luck. Such is the kindness of strangers in difficult times.

In the days that followed, he kept out of sight and ate in nondescript cafés, blended in with crowds. He had become invisible, unknown like his writing. Every day in borrowed rooms from old friends, he added pages to his new novel. Unwillingly, he had become the hero of his story. He used the word reluctantly and with some disdain. There was always an antagonist who dogged and interrupted the life of his protagonists. There was always someone or something to overcome. He didn't have a clue who the antagonist was. He was real, and he felt his presence as he closed in on him.

Now Russia has proclaimed that it is going to pull back and concentrate its forces in the Donbas region, to *liberate* it. Putin will place a willing boob to be the head of the new state who will ask Russia for recognition and military support. This will allow Putin to announce a victory. No nation should acquiesce to this farce. Russia will still continue to bomb and terrorize the rest of the country, killing many people and displacing millions from their homes.

This afternoon, Manuel felt as though someone was following him. He was in a crowd of pedestrians crossing Bloor Street at Yonge. He was certain he had seen this person before, maybe yesterday. Six feet, thin, dark glasses, and a blue windbreaker over a white shirt. Manuel went left on Bloor on the north side then up Belair then turned left onto Cumberland. He crossed over and stopped to look at a store window. There he was in the reflection looking at him. He upped his pace and went over to Yorkville then to Hazelton Avenue and into the indoor shopping mall where he lost the person in the maze of stores then exited onto Avenue Road. It was almost too easy, that is, unless the person was just going to the mall to buy a new shirt.

As he walked, he wondered how much more of this he could take. He felt that he was going to have to confront someone soon. Put his back against the wall. Take him down.

Manuel called a friend from the old days, Rafael, who lived in a condo on Logan Avenue. "Sure," he said, "come on over. We'll order *lahmajoun*." Rafael welcomed Manuel with a hug and a kiss on the cheek. When the food arrived, he heated the *lahmajoun,* the Armenian pizzas topped with spiced lamb, onions and parsley, tomatoes and peppers, then placed the plates on the table along with bowls of yogurt, onions and cucumbers. Manuel confessed that he had nowhere to go. "Of course, you can stay here," Rafael said. "We have a lot to catch up on. All that stuff in the seventies and eighties we were involved in." As they talked late into the night, Rafael had left the television on so that they could see the bombs and missiles that were striking the outskirts of Kyiv and destroying Mariupol which was still being levelled by the *brave* Russian Army. Rafael sat back shaking his head. "Can you believe this?" He hesitated a moment then brought up what had happened at Orly Airport and the embassy in Ottawa. "We're a lot older now," Rafael said slightly inebriated.

"Yes, but not much wiser. Not much has changed, Rafael."

As he prepared for bed, Manuel received a call from Aaron. "How are you holding up?"

"Okay for now."

"I got a call from a contact in foreign affairs in Ottawa. Apparently, there is an issue over your father's manuscripts and papers."

"That's a new one. Never heard that before."

"The Director of the National Library of the republic has a letter written by your father stating that he is leaving all his writing and books to them."

"He never told me about this. What should I do?"

"Do you want all of your father's material to go there? Is that where it should end up? Do you wish to contest this?"

"Maybe. I need to think about this. Is the guy coming to stake his claim and take everything back?"

"Don't know. Why else would he come all this way? Think about this and what you want to do about it. We can see how strong his claim is. Do you have anything from your father making you his literary executor?"

"Under the circumstances, I can't really return home, right now. Perhaps he left me a letter. Let me think; call me tomorrow. Thanks for the heads up. Good night."

The past had returned with a vengeance. Manuel knew he would have to keep his wits about him. As he slid under the covers, he thought, someone really wants to cancel me. What should I do? Now the republic wants to take my father's legacy from me. Does it belong to me, or should it be given to the people about whom he wrote so passionately?

It seemed that more and more was being taken from him. He looked up and saw the images on the television. Groups of innocent women, men and children were scrambling in a panic out of a burned and blackened apartment building that had just been hit by a missile. They stood in stunned silence in the middle of the road that was covered with chunks of cement and all sorts of debris from inside the apartment block, their private lives destroyed and exposed. Some turned in circles; some cried; others were yelling. Two men carried a grandmother out of the blasted building on a kitchen chair. A blank expression was frozen on her face. Blood ran out of her ears. All were

victims. All cared for each other. Manuel shouted
in his mind *Death to tyrants*!

8

Manuel stayed at Rafael's for a few days, reminiscing. He didn't tell him about his problems. There was no need to burden him. Each night they sat transfixed in front of the television, hoping for an intervention against Russia. None was coming.

Late at night after the Russian flagship missile carrier *Moskva* sank, Manuel returned home. At first, he felt uncomfortable as he wasn't certain he had a home. He entered and looked around. Nothing had changed. He sat in his library with the lights off, wondering who or what was waiting for him. Hours later, as the sun rose and cast its light through the windows, he saw his surroundings and was comforted. It felt good to be in his own space among his books and papers. He went to his bedroom and fell into a peaceful sleep.

At 11 am he woke. When he rose, he found himself disoriented and unsure why he was at home. After breakfast, he took his cup of coffee and went to the front window. The familiar façades across the street and the sight of his neighbours watching their children play on their lawns felt known, normal. When he looked left down the street, he noticed a grey Chevy, a new model but plain like a government car. The driver was still sitting behind the wheel, playing with the radio tuner then picked up his phone and spoke for what seemed like a long time. Manuel went out on the balcony and stared down at the guy. Suddenly, the driver glanced up at him then put down his phone. A few minutes later, a woman came out of the building a few doors down from his, opened the car door and slid in next to him. An animated discussion ensued with hands waving. They pulled away but not before they both looked back at him. Manuel had to check himself. What person hasn't been annoyed when waiting in a car for his partner? He likely called her to tell her that they were going to be late. Maybe. Okay, he thought, but why has my phone service been on and off intermittently? When it worked, he heard clicks on the speaker. He made a note to buy a burner phone.

Later that morning in the shower as he washed the soap off his body, he noticed that his skin had changed. It had become puffy in places. Bumps, bruises, and scars stood out. Nothing seemed to heal quickly anymore. His skin didn't shine in the light as it used to. It was dull, almost lifeless. Running around trying to stay ahead of the malevolent force out to get him had given him aches and pains in his hips and back. He now walked with a slight limp in his right leg. Everything had become an effort. At sixty-seven what could he expect?

Manuel spent the rest of the morning rereading his father's memoirs. He was amazed at the way his father had been able to cross boundaries comfortably. His compatriots had a long history of being dragomen, linguistic middlemen, who were familiar enough with several cultures which allowed them to facilitate communication and commerce among people who would not normally be able to do so. His father had known several languages well and was a comfortable and skillful go-between. There was so much that had been destroyed by the genocide, but his father had retained the memory of his father and his neighbours dealing with American, British, and French government people and missionaries passing through who required their assistance which they were glad to provide for a fee. Stories were told that were taken back to Europe and North America, but none were able to prevent the coming slaughter. Even in his new home in Toronto, his father seemed to move effortlessly across borders and in between the many cultures in the city. He admired this in his father and realized that he did not have his skill. Contrary to his father, he inhabited the borderlands between loneliness and community. His life resembled a form of self-banishment that fed off a refusal of roots, something his father had chastised him for. "Why do you deny where you came from?" he often asked him. "We are the inheritors of a rich heritage." Manuel recalled on one occasion during such a discussion he had said, "It's all too tragic. Death and sorrow are an oppressive burden to live with." His father had stared at him and held back his anger. "Your desire not to engage with your heritage through me has alienated you. Perhaps you are humiliated by it. This has made you powerless, perhaps even guilty." It was a moment that Manuel had never forgotten. "My son, you have become a liminal man. You seem to take comfort existing in these in-between spaces. What is preventing you from crossing over and into?"

The constant feeling of unease and the added tension of being pursued made his future seem doubtful. He appeared to be at a moment of transition in his life, at the threshold leading to the unknown. He felt he was always on the verge of something, a precipice. It was palpable, but he had no idea what was waiting for him.

He returned to his library and looked at the rows of books on the shelves that both he and his father had collected over many years. His father's desk, which he now used as his own, had his pens and papers spread out as well as bottles of ink. This was the context of his life and the place where he most felt his purpose. Why then these intense feelings of restlessness, disquiet, and apprehension? Another step closer to the edge, a step away.

He picked up one of his father's texts, "Orphan Boy, Orphan Man," written in 1975. The dedication read "To My wife, Marie, who gave life meaning." His mother had died in 1970 at the young age of fifty-five. His father had felt her loss deeply for the remainder of his life. Manuel too adored her. She had given him so much love and care. When he came to her with a crazy idea, she would say, "Really, my son. Think carefully about this for two days then come back and we'll discuss it." She had been the voice of reason that kept them together even after the arguments he had had with his father.

After reading his father's essay, he understood that his father saw his ethnic and cultural identities as his main frames of identity. Since the genocide and the destruction, they allowed him to build his identity and reconnect with his culture, that sense of right that each community lives by. His cultural identity had become essential to his personal identity and the way he related to the world. In the third paragraph, he had written the following. "After having been placed in a series of orphanages, each one further away from my home, I went where the world was taking me. I was in exile, a diaspora person, in search for a place that no longer knew me or wanted me. A choice lay before me. I could either rail against the injustice and hope that in some way my writing would be a way of keeping the memories of many of my compatriots alive and of spreading what they suffered for being who they were, or I could be one of the many unknowns whose silence has been swallowed by history." When he turned the page, a slip of paper fell to the floor. He picked it up. His father had written a note in blue-black ink with his fountain pen. "Use this from Aeschylus as an epigraph. 'In the heart is no sleep; there drips instead pain that remembers wounds.'"

9

Anxiety-filled days and nightmarish, sleepless nights. Mariupol is surrounded by Russian forces. Putin continues to bombard and pulverize the ghost city. Only a handful of soldiers remain deep inside the steel mill along with women and children. Reptilian Putin smiles on tv and says that he might use a new bomb on them even though it hasn't been fully tested yet. He refuses to open a humanitarian corridor to allow those inside to leave. He says he will; then when buses arrive to take the frightened people away, he doesn't permit it. He's like a mad Nazi scientist wanting to try a new poison gas on those inside the shower room who are holding their breaths as they stare at the vents on the concrete ceiling. In the end, starving Russians will attack the Kremlin and will tear him and his beasts apart, skin and muscle and sinew from their corrupt bones, shrieking their starved madness. They will stare at their blood covered clothes, yet it won't be enough for them all to pay for what they have done.

Manuel got out of bed and went to the washroom to splash cold water on his face. Morning was still hours away. He went to the library and turned on his computer and forced himself to work through the anger and fear that someone was closing in on him. When the desktop glowed on the screen, he saw that his message icon indicated that someone had contacted him. He clicked on it and saw that it was from Aaron.

Manuel, I hope you're well and safe. My contact in Canadian security services called me. The *Direction générale de la sécurité extérieure*, France's equivalent to the CSIS, had put out a watch on you since the Orly airport attack on July 15, 1983. For some reason they have reinstituted the watch on you. Do you know any reason why this might be? You're not involved in anything are you? You're being watched. I wouldn't be surprised if they bring you in for questioning. If that happens, call me immediately. Keep low and safe. I should be back soon. Aaron.

Manuel went to the shelf on which he kept all his yearly agendas. He found 1983 and flipped to July 15, 1983. That was 39 years ago, he thought. He was writing a paper on Louis-Ferdinand Céline and was working at the *Bibliothèque Nationale* in Paris. He remembered reading about the attack. It had been in the news for days. Armenian militants had bombed the Turkish Airlines counter at Orly Airport in the city to bring about recognition of the Armenian Genocide as well as to claim reparations for the crime. He recalled that his father had called him to make sure he was safe but also to get his reaction. When there was none that would satisfy him, his father simply said, be safe and ended the call. But why now after all these years? His father would have said, "Because genocide never ends, my son. It destroys generations and demands a continuous response." His father wanted him to recognize the need for a call to action. At the time, Manuel had been interested in Céline, finishing his paper and having it peer reviewed then published. That was his future. Bombs at Orly was about his father's past. When his father read this in Manuel's letter to him, he nearly collapsed in anger. This can't be my son, he thought. He took the letter and placed it in a folder and slammed it closed.

Years later, his father had called him into the library in order to discuss the lack of reparations for the Armenian survivors after the Genocide. He showed him a text written by Simon Vratsian, the last Prime Minister of the First Republic of Armenia, titled "The Armenian Nuremberg," published in 1991.

"A quarter of a century later, after World War II, in conditions very much the same, an international court-martial was held in Nuremberg for Nazi criminals. The Nazi leaders were executed, and the German people were made to pay an indemnity to Jews, to calm the indignant conscience of the 'civilized humanity.' Different was the attitude of that same 'civilized humanity' with regard to Armenians. One half of the Armenian population of Turkey had been massacred in a most vicious way, the other half had been scattered all over the world. The property of Armenians was stolen. Towns and villages were deserted. And when the time arrived for indemnity, the 'civilized humanity' remained unconcerned. The Armenians organized, with the 'sacred blood of their sons' their own Armenian Nuremberg for the Turk butchers."

"Why did you spend time on Céline?" his father had shouted at him. "He had written anti-Semitic polemical tracts and wanted France to form an alliance with Nazi Germany." Manuel stepped back as he feared his father was going to attack him. "You need to explain yourself, Manuel."

Manuel motioned for his father to sit at his desk. He walked around and faced him. "In Céline's world, there is no moral order. Those in power will always suppress the poor and the weak. Yes, he was a pessimist and believed that the human condition was for most of us one of suffering and that there was nothing after death. What's left but to struggle in this harsh world?" His father shook his head. "You are a defiant one, my son. It's a pity we never worked together. We might have accomplished things for our cause."

Manuel went to his father still seated and hugged him. "There are many causes and many ways."

Over the next two weeks, Manuel had tried to contact Aaron several times each without success. He had left several voice messages for him using coded language no one else would understand. "This is your hockey buddy. Give me a call. I want to discuss the team trades and the chances in the upcoming season." There was no return call from him. He went by Aaron's home at night to see if there were lights on besides those he had left lit before leaving. All was as he had left them, and there was no movement inside.

Now another week had gone by without a word from his friend. He called Aaron's office ostensibly to make an appointment. His secretary had not received any word from him. She had called the conference site in Paris and the hotel where he had been staying. Nothing. Aaron seemed to have disappeared. This was most unusual, for Aaron was a lawyer with an excellent reputation. His secretary intimated that everyone was worried. Manuel ran through the possibilities. Is he having a quiet affair with someone in Paris? Possibly, however, given the serious nature of his work, it wasn't likely that he would disappear without a word. Then there was the chance that he had been kidnapped. Given that he had been making inquiries into Manuel's security situation might have triggered a response; one of the services could have brought him in for questioning. That was quite likely. Manuel wondered how he could inquire into his friend's safety without compromising himself. He drew the drapes tighter across the windows then pulled out the chair his father had sat on for many years and let himself fall onto it. Without Aaron, he truly felt alone in the increasingly hostile world. He took out a blank sheet of paper and unscrewed the cap of his fountain pen and continued writing his novel.

10

Two agonizing weeks later on a bright sunny Monday morning, Manuel was sitting at his desk thinking of how he could move his story forward when his phone rang. He didn't recognize the number and wasn't certain if he should touch the red button to engage. What the hell, he thought, it might be information he needed. When he did, the person hung up before he could say a word. After a brief silence, he put his head down and continued reading his manuscript. The phone rang again. This time, he picked up his cell phone and connected right away. He heard the person breathing.

"Hello," he said softly.

"Hello," was the firm response. A woman's voice. "Is this Aaron's friend?"

"Yes, it is. Who is this?"

"Not on the phone. We have to meet."

"Yes. Where?"

"At the ROM. Stand in front of the Torah Case from the Ming-Qing Dynasty from the synagogue in Kaifeng, China. It's in the Bishop

White Gallery. Be there at two pm. Wear something red so I can recognize you."

She abruptly shut down communication. He noted her number in the recent call log, but it might have been a fake number. Manuel had three hours to get ready. He was anxious to find out about Aaron and if he had more news for him. He wondered about the woman he was going to meet. Was it a trap?

He got ready and took the subway to the Museum station, exited and walked up Queen's Park then climbed the stairs of the Weston entrance to the building. He worked his way through the first level, stopping at certain moments to observe the displays before entering the Gallery of Chinese Temple Art. It was moderately crowded. Several groups had gathered in front of the displays and paintings. As he looked around, he tried putting a face to the voice on the phone with little success. Finally, he put on a red scarf and walked around the gallery. He had prepared himself to run in case this was a set-up. It wouldn't be easy with the pain in his right leg. He felt the eyes of women upon him as he circled the area. He stopped and stood before the immense wall painting, *The Paradise of Maitreya* dated 1298 AD, depicting Maitreya, the Buddha of the future and successor to the historical Buddha, enthroned in heaven and awaiting his incarnation on earth where he will save the souls of lost humanity. If I had a soul, Manuel thought, it would definitely need saving. As he looked up at the large painting, he felt a gentle hand touch his shoulder. "Manuel?" she asked softly. "Aaron's friend?" Manuel turned and saw a tall dark-complexioned woman, with long dark hair pulled back. "I'm Ana Leckta. Buy me a coffee." She curled her arm under his and began to lead him out of the museum. Somewhat startled, Manuel went with her.

As she turned and guided him towards one of the corridors, she noticed a museum guard walking towards them. She turned again and circled the large display at the centre of the gallery to shield them. She hurried Manuel towards another corridor leading out to the main hall then stopped.

"What's going on?" Manuel asked.

"They're on to us. Just follow me."

Two more guards in blue blazers stopped at the entrance to the gallery. Ana looked around and found the door against the west wall. The floor plan was correct. She slow walked Manuel towards it. Small black letters on the solid oak offered a chance. **Private**. Ana suddenly jerked to her left and pointed to a corner of the painting of the Buddha. The guards followed her gaze and stepped forward to get a better look at what she was indicating. While their attention was distracted, Ana swiftly moved to the oak door, opened it and disappeared inside a small dark room, pulling Manuel along with her.

"How did you know?"

"I know a lot of things, Manuel. Just trust me."

On the computer screen in the control room on the main floor behind the display of medieval swords and axes, Emre Avci, the afternoon security P3 scratched his balding head. "Where could they have gone?" Allen Dreyfus, one of the computer techs was confused. "They just disappeared." Emre Avci shot a look at him. "You mean, where could they have gone, sir?" The young tech corrected himself. "Where might they be, oh, my Captain?" A satisfied smile crossed his small, pinched face. "Better, Dreyfus, much better. I know exactly where they're going. We will trap them and take them in. Call Ottawa." Dreyfus was at a loss to know what his captain wanted him to do. Emre Avci raised his voice. "Time is crucial here. Call CSIS to tell them we have the person they're looking for trapped in our museum. The number is on my desk in large black numbers. Ask to speak to Director Esterhazy. He will know. Then send out an all-museum alert to watch for Manuel Sweet, as he calls himself now. Back home, in my country, he is still known as Shirinian." Dreyfus looked up at his captain. "You said you knew where he was going, sir." Emre Avci smiled and put his hands on his black leather belt and squeezed it as he used to do when he was a cadet at the *Kara Harp Okulu*, the Turkish Military Academy in Ankara, where he had trained to be a commissioned officer in the Turkish Army. He liked the feel and smell of his leather belts and boots and often stood in front of the mirror in his room in full uniform, admiring himself before a parade. An unfortunate incident he was involved in forced him to leave the academy before receiving his commission. His family was shamed and disowned him. Avci immigrated to Argentina but couldn't find work; then after a series of false starts and bouts of circular thinking, he ended up in Canada where a distant uncle found him a job with the cleaning staff at the Royal Ontario Museum in Toronto, where he had been languishing in Little Beirut on Lawrence Avenue. He was ambitious and used his very modest military background to get a position in the security section. After a year, he considered himself to be the de facto head of the tech section for which he had no training. He insisted that the two techs who worked with him, Allen Dreyfus and Ross Kalnikoff, call him captain because of his so-called military training. This amused them, but they went along with the illusion. They knew that if any blame came down on them, the captain would be responsible.

As Ana Leckta led Manuel through the utility corridors of the museum, Manuel stopped her. "Can you tell me what's going on? How do you know Aaron? How is he? Where is he?"

"Keep your voice down. We don't want them to track us. Aaron is fine. He's in Paris getting information that can help get you free of the mess you got yourself into on July 15, 1983. Remember? You were researching at the National Library. And agencies have been tracking you ever since. It's coming to a head now."

Dumbfounded, Manuel asked, "What mess? You mean Orly? Who are you?"

"It's too long to explain now. If we get out of this, I might tell you if you buy me an expensive dinner." Now, listen carefully. Security will think that you will go to the tattoo exhibition on the third floor. It's titled "TATTOO: RITUAL, IDENTITY, OBSESSION, ART."

"Why would they think that?"

"Come on. You know why. During the deportations of Armenians to the Syrian desert, each time a group approached Turkish or Kurdish towns or villages, the locals stole Armenian children and used them as servants or wives. Many others were sold as slaves and given a tattoo. The boys and girls were force converted to Islam and were assimilated into Turkish or Kurdish families.

A League of Nations Report estimates that 30,000 Armenian girls were sold in slave markets to go to harems or to be used as slave labour. Today, there are many Turkish and Kurdish families with hidden Armenian grandmothers. In Turkey, they are called "remnants of the sword." Who knows how many Armenian orphans survived but were Turkified and assimilated?

"Yes, I knew some of this. But how did you?"

"Not now. Follow me. We're going out a side door and will amble along Philosopher's Walk, just as you use to do years ago going to your office at the university. Some say that life's a circle. I see it as a series of arcs marking the changes in one's life as one rises then falls. The mystery is where and how we end up. Take my arm and let's take a leisurely stroll like two lovers. Come. Shortly, you will take me to dinner."

11

At Harbord Street, near the back campus of University College, Ana Leckta hailed a cab and told the driver to head east along Bloor Street to Danforth and Chester. Manuel sat back leaning tight against Ana, unsure if he should trust her. He whispered a few words to her, but she shook her head and whispered in his ear. "Not now." Twenty-five minutes later, the cab stopped on Danforth just east of Chester and let them off. She took Manuel's hand and guided him along the sidewalk. "I know an excellent restaurant just up here. *Smyrna*. Do you know it?"

"I don't think so," he mumbled.

"You'll like it. They make food that will be familiar to you, food like your mother made."

"My mother grew up in France, but her family was from Smyrna. She never knew them. What made you think I knew the origins of my mother's food?"

"I know a lot of things." She interrupted him. "You're going to have to learn to trust me."

She opened the door for him and followed him in. The owner saw them and came over to her with a smile beaming under his large, bushy, grey-black moustache. He kissed her on both cheeks and engaged in a short conversation at the end of which he said, *Nai, fysika.* "The table in the corner. I'll see you won't be disturbed." She tried to calm Manuel when they sat. "Don't worry; Tasso's a friend." Manuel looked around the room. It was narrow but extended far back towards the kitchen where two chefs were busy preparing food. Waiters carrying large plates of kebab and *brizola sto fourno* moved expertly among the wooden tables randomly placed in the room, each surrounded by wooden chairs. Pictures and photographs dotted the white stucco walls, including one next to where they were seated titled, *The Burning of Smyrna in September 1922.* "You see," she said.

"Those terrible events marked the end of the cosmopolitan city that was home to Greeks, Armenians, Turks, and Jews as well as other groups," she said. "Smyrna became singularly Turkish. My family was from Smyrna. My mother Miriam was Jewish, my father Athanasios Greek. My grandmother Lea told my mother the story of the disaster, and she passed it down to me. I'm from there in the same way you are. In our hearts we're Smyrniot."

"I know the story only too well," Manuel told her. My maternal grandmother's family was on that quay, hoping to get on a boat that would take them to one of the five French warships that were anchored in the harbour. Everything burned around them. They became refugees."

"That's why you're here, and that's the reason I'm here."

"Really," Manuel said. He looked at Ana and saw that in the soft light of the restaurant, her sharp features had given way to a subtler presence. "You were going to tell me about yourself," he said. "We both have roots in Smyrna. So, who is Ana Leckta?"

Ana looked over to Tasso. "Ouzo, *para kalo*." Tasso went to the bar and returned, carrying a tray with a bottle of ouzo, two small glasses and a carafe of water. Ana poured two shots out and lifted her glass. *Stin ygeia sas.* Cheers." She drank and put down her glass. "This will make things easier."

"For whom?" he asked and downed the ouzo. He felt it slide down his throat, releasing an anise bomb in his mouth.

"Both of us, but mostly you. Do you know the Greek poet, Cavafy?"

"I've read some of his work in translation."

"Do you know his poem, "Ithaca"?

"I do," Manuel said.

"It begins," Ana recited,

> *When you start on your journey to Ithaca,*
> *then pray that the road is long,*
> *full of adventure, full of knowledge.*

"and ends," Manuel continued,

> *With the great wisdom you have gained,*
> *with so much experience,*

you must surely have understood by then
what Ithaca means.

"Well, if this is my journey," he said, "I don't think I have understood very much."

"Things will become clearer to you."

"I sense you're telling me I have to suffer more. After pain comes knowledge. Well, Ana Leckta, someone is after me, wants me to disappear. I want to know why. I'm prepared to suffer but for what?"

"I want to help you understand your father. I want to be on this journey with you."

"Who are you?" he asked sharply. "How do you know me? How do you know Aaron?"

"I work with him at times. He calls me when he's confronted with a particularly difficult and confusing situation. He's worried about you."

"So, you know that I'm in difficult circumstances. Where is he?"

She refilled the glasses with more ouzo and added a small quantity of water that turned the alcohol cloudy.

"In Paris." She savoured the anise liquid.

"Is he still at the conference?"

"Drink and I will tell you."

He drained his glass. His mind turned into a flavoured haze.

"No, it's over. There's a possibility that we may have to travel to meet him."

"In Paris?"

"Yes, perhaps elsewhere."

"I still have no idea who you are."

"Be content that I am here to aid you."

"How can you?"

She smiled. "I read. I study. I have a photographic memory. I retain everything. I gather scraps others have left on the floor. It's a gift and at times a curse. I have become a miscellany, a group, a collection of different items, a mixture."

"Like being from Smyrna," he said.

"Yes, the same way you are. In this way, I can help you."

Manuel was as confused as ever. "Did Aaron send you?"

"It doesn't matter. He knows I'm here."

It was as if a veil had been drawn over his eyes. He began to struggle as he formulated the question. "So, what do we do next?"

"We drink ouzo and eat. The rest will follow."

"Well, Ana Leckta, I will follow you."

12

Ana curled her arm around Manuel's as they walked tipsy together into the night. The hint of intimacy stirred feelings he hadn't felt in some time. He had had girlfriends over the years, even a long relationship with a colleague that ended up with them living together. Eventually, love and companionship turned into debates and finally hostility as neither partner was willing to change positions and see the good in the other and the benefit of their being together. After two years, it ended. One snowy night in November when he returned home after researching at the library, he opened the front door and went to the kitchen where he uncorked the bottle of Pinot Noir he had just purchased and pulled back the lid on a vegetarian pizza from *Pizza Padre*. He listened for her footsteps upstairs, but there was no sound. He called her name. There was no voice but his own. He went to their bedroom to see her, but she was gone. All she had left was a letter on his pillow. "Two years wasted with you. Don't write; don't phone." In the end, he thought, everyone disappears. Where do we all go?

"It's just here," Ana said to the cabby. She turned to Manuel. "It's an older condo but living near the east-west subway line is very convenient; I don't drive." It was a solid, well-maintained, low-rise dark-red brick building. Ana lived on the fifth floor in a large three-bedroom unit whose walls were lined with bookcases and filing cabinets. "I couldn't move even if I wanted to," she said. "My life is too full of information." Manuel thought her mind must be as crammed as her living space.

She went to the linen closet and took out sheets, a blanket, and pillows. "It's the couch for you. It's not safe for you to return home, not until we figure this out. I'll go out for coffee and croissants before you wake. I've put a blue towel out for you in the bathroom. Goodnight."

With that, Ana went to her bedroom and closed the door. Manuel heard her computer boot up. He closed his eyes, "She's going to fix my life." After the adventure they had had at the museum and their escape, he fell into a deep sleep, thinking of Ana and how beautiful she was becoming. In the dark, he saw Ana walking with him along la rue Franque on the quay in Smyrna. She leaned her head on his shoulder. An ouzo bomb burst in his mind.

The sound of waves gently lapping the sandy shore at Cavendish Beach that summer years ago when his father had taken the family on a seaside vacation in the Maritimes. Manuel was stretched out on a lounge chair warmed by the afternoon sun. His father was swimming with his mother before the immensity of the Atlantic Ocean. There wasn't a cloud in the summer sky. Not a worry. Not a care in the world. All he had to do was grow up; his parents would take care of everything. His mind drifted. There was nothing tying him to Orly or anything. That day in July 1983 he was researching at the Bibliothèque Nationale. After a good morning's work, he had gone to a nearby café and sat at a table on the terrace and ordered a coffee. He had already explained all this to Aaron. He had remained on the terrace and drunk two cups of coffee and had gone over his notes from the morning's research. Why did his father always chastise him for not getting more involved? He had often told him that my history is also your history. You can't escape it. That day in Paris sitting at the café, Manuel knew he must leave Paris. It was time to disappear.

Ana touched Manuel's shoulder and gently shook him. His eyes opened as the aroma of the coffee that Ana had brought filled the room. "Good morning, lazy bones. I hope you had a good sleep." He rubbed his eyes and smiled. "I did, thank you." She was a beautiful woman in her late forties, olive skinned from her Greek and Jewish heritage, slender and only slightly shorter than he was. He sat up. His head was still spinning from remembering that summer in Paris as it always did. She held his hand and helped him rise. He was surprised to see that someone who spent most of her time reading was in remarkably good shape. She smiled as she understood the expression on his face. "Yes, I do work out. You should too. It will come in handy if we want sort out your problem."

"Is there anything in the papers this morning?"

She shook her head. "Aaron called very early this morning."

"Does he have any leads?" he asked anxiously.

"He was going to meet a couple of contacts. He'll get back to us. Meanwhile, he suggested we stay inside."

"Suits me," he said. "I need time to figure this out."

They sat at a small table next to a bookshelf full of nautical charts and books on tides and ocean currents around the world. "If we need to sail, I've got us covered," she said. "That's comforting," he replied and drank his coffee. When Manuel took a bite of his croissant, he was instantly transported back to the café near the Bibliothèque Nationale on the day of the attack at Orly Airport. His breath was suddenly sucked out of him as if an explosion had gone off nearby.

"You look pale. Are you okay?"

"It's just…there's a lot to deal with. I'm okay."

She put her hand on his. "Let's go over a few things. Tell me about your father."

"My father?"

"It will be helpful. I've read everything he published. I want to know about the man, your father."

Manuel thought for a moment. How much should he tell her? How much did he want to divulge? Who is Ana Leckta that she should care?

"I understand your hesitation. You don't know me, but we've had a similar background. I know your profile. You had a somewhat difficult relationship with your father as I did with mine. That generation went through hell and came out having to repair the damage. You and I are the result."

Feeling relieved by her willingness to open up to him, he spoke. "My father was obsessed with making the Genocide known and holding the guilty criminally responsible. It was never enough for him."

Ana put her cup on the table. "We moved from Athens to Paris where my father was a journalist. I want to say that he was a loving father, but he was often absent covering stories. Even when we were in the same room, he would retreat within himself and became unreachable. He was so committed to humanitarian causes. He had lost most of his family in Smyrna. The ghosts followed him into exile. My mother and I adapted. When he was present in the moment, he was a good father, but the memories of what he lived through took him from us. He was killed while working on a story in Libya. If we're not fighting for human rights, what are we?"

"Would you believe that my father often berated me for not following him along his path. He wasn't willing to grant me the freedom to choose my own. Even after I became a professor of literature and had made a name for myself, he would tell me, 'This is how you pay the debt owed? There's so much we have to do.' All I could say was that I had the right to live my life my way. 'Yes,' he would answer, 'just as all those murdered had the right to live, but not doing anything to right the wrong is an insult to them.' Then there were times when he was gentle, kind in his words, inquisitive about my research and writing. Living with the ups and downs was difficult. Eventually, I had to move out."

Ana took his hand. "Genocide never ends with the killing. The pain and anguish burn their way through generations."

"My father was right, and I'm right. There doesn't seem to be a satisfactory response for either. There must be justice, and there must be peace, life without the oppression of the past."

"Maybe not for some in this world, Manuel."

"How did you get into doing what you do, Ana?"

"Because of my *gift*, I entered university earlier than I should have and finished a doctorate by the time I was twenty-three. The American government offered me a job. You can guess which branch. I didn't want to become a slave; so I refused. Besides, I wanted to stay in Canada and help people fight government overreach. That's how I met Aaron. I've worked with him a lot, but I'm a freelancer. Aaron told me about your problem before he left for Paris. I have something for you. You're not going to be happy."

They finished their breakfast and cleared the table. "Let me show you what I found last night." She went to her office and returned with two printed sheets. "I found these on a government security website in France I broke into. I did two separate searches, your name and Orly attack July 15, 1983. Here's what showed up, a photo of you drinking coffee at a café near the old *Bibliothèque Nationale*, and one of the damages at the Turkish Airlines counter at Orly Airport just after the bomb went off."

Manuel was shocked. "So much damage. But why did they take a photo of me at the café?"

"There were security cameras everywhere. Even back then."

"Well, it proves I couldn't have been involved at the airport. I was miles away at the time."

"A report written by an investigator went into your father's past. He wrote about your father's *activisme extrémiste* and surmised that you must share his opinions. Otherwise, he asks, what were you doing in Paris that day? He concludes that it wasn't a coincidence. From that moment, a watch was put out on you. The notice was relayed to Canadian security services. They concurred and acted upon it."

"So, for thirty-nine years, that has been on me. I've been watched and followed, suspected all this time. Why did this come to a head now?"

"There was a strong chance that the President of Turkey was going to make an official diplomatic visit this year. They were taking precautions by putting a watch on you to see if you are implicated in any way with known anti-Turkish groups."

Manuel was trembling with rage. "I had absolutely nothing to do with this!"

"We have to find out if there's anything else," Ana said. "I didn't get much sleep last night. I need to rest." She sat on the sofa and closed her eyes. "You know, in all these years, I've never had anyone I've really felt for. You, Manuel, I feel I've known you all my life." He sat beside her and leaned back. They both drifted off.

Two hours later, Manuel woke with a start. He stood up and looked around. He rubbed his eyes then went through the apartment looking for Ana but couldn't find her. On the kitchen table he saw a note she had left. "It's 12:05. I've gone across the street for some food for us. I'll be back shortly."

He went back to the grey sofa with the soft cushions where he kneeled and looked out the window. He checked his watch. She had been gone for only fifteen minutes. Looking at the row of grocery stores across the road on Danforth Avenue East, he saw her exit *M. Gandhi's Fruit & Veg*, holding a small bag. When she stopped for a moment to look at other items on the display tables outside, he went to put on his shoes to go and meet her. By the time he looked out the window again, she was no longer there. He scanned the street but couldn't find her. Perhaps she had gone to another store, he thought. But there was no sign of her. Surely, he thought, she must be on her way up. He opened the door to her apartment which made a loud groaning sound. He listened carefully for the elevator. It wasn't in use. Back in the apartment, he instinctively closed the blinds and peeked out from the bottom right corner. His phone suddenly lit up with a message. "I'm being followed. Get out now! Don't try to contact me. I'll text you later. A. L." Manuel quickly gathered his things and went down the back stairs to the rear entrance, holding onto the railing because of his sore leg. At the main floor he exited and hurried past the blue and green recycling bins. His phone lit up again. Ana had sent him a photo of one of the two men she believed were stalking her. He had blond hair and wore a pale green jacket. Manuel saw that the man's right eyelid drooped significantly. He took back garden paths until he was far away from Ana's place. He felt pangs of guilt leaving her. Maybe there was no one after Ana. She was being cautious. Given all she's been through, she will know what to do. No doubt, she will call later. I'll go back, and we'll have a quiet supper together. I want to see her again. He felt safe with her. He wanted to tell her that, but he was sure she knew. He took many streets south, then more east then back north and ended up on Coxwell Avenue near Michael Garron Hospital. Finally, he stopped at a bus shelter on the corner of Mortimer Avenue to catch his breath and figure out what to do. His legs and back were sore from walking quickly. His chest was heaving. At his age, he knew he couldn't maintain this pace. His phone lit up again. It was from Ana. Then it went dead. That's troublesome, he mumbled. Stress began to take its toll. He sat back on the uncomfortable aluminum seat. A bus stopped to pick up the only passenger waiting in the shelter. He shook his head indicating he wasn't waiting for the bus. Manuel could see the driver's mouth offer an opinion as he closed the bus door and sped off in a cloud of dust. He sat alone in the dirty bus shelter with one broken plastic window and graffiti covering the others. He needed to hear from Ana. He felt frozen in time, not able to move. Hours later, he felt his chin fall onto his chest and saw the last light being sucked out of the day. All went quiet and peaceful.

13

Nothing. He had not received a word from Ana. Was she on the run? Had she been taken in? All he had was the clothes he was wearing and his knapsack which contained his laptop and two large capacity solid state drives which held all of his father's writing and a first draft of his new novel, a notebook and a pouch of pens and pencils. In one of the deep pockets, were his set of keys which would allow him entry into his home which no doubt would be dangerous. He kept his phone off then turned it on and left it in a garbage bin in the busy lobby of the hospital on Coxwell Avenue. Manuel went south then east. Now there was no way anyone could communicate with him or find him. He felt the loneliness in the pit of his stomach.

He still had money but knew going to a hotel would be risky. An hour later after a long walk, he found himself back at Rafael's place on Logan Avenue. Rafael welcomed him like a brother and prepared a meal. "You look hungry and tired,

Manny. Go have a shower. We'll eat when you're ready."

They sat at the table Rafael had set and raised their glasses. Rafael asked, "Tell me Manny, are you on the run?"

"I am, but I don't know why. I think someone from Canadian Security Services is after me."

"What for? Something you wrote?"

Manuel wondered if he should tell what he knows to his friend. He didn't want to get him involved but needed to unburden himself. "The government thinks I was involved in the attack at Orly Airport in 1983."

"That's crazy. They caught the guys who did it. How could they think you were part of it."

"This is the insane part. You know how strong my father's writing was. They analyzed it then discovered that I was in Paris at the same time, researching at the *Bibliothèque Nationale*. They even have a photo of me having a coffee at a café near the library the same afternoon of the attack. They put two and two together and figured I was part of it. Maybe even that my father had put me up to it. They've been trying to get me for a while now. Now two friends who were helping me have disappeared."

"You need a lawyer."

"I have one, a good friend, who was checking on things in France. I haven't heard from him for several days. Also, a woman researcher who was helping me here has disappeared. I really liked her. I fear I'm next; I know it."

"Turn your phone off."

"I threw it away."

"You can stay here as long as you want. Don't go out. Let things calm down. Give me the contact information of your two friends. I'll make some discreet inquiries tomorrow. Let's enjoy a meal first; then you can give me the details. I'll grill some salmon and get another bottle of Sauvignon Blanc. In the meantime, let's take our minds off this; tell me about your new novel."

"That's fiction, Rafael. I control what's happening on the page. Someone bad is controlling this situation."

Having found a peaceful haven at his friend's home, Manuel tuned out his worries and focused on his novel. On the third day of his stay, he finished two new chapters. He went out on the balcony and let the sun warm his face. The air was sweet with the scents of flowers, basil, oregano, and sage that Rafael had grown in pots. Manuel leaned on the metal fence and heard the sound from his laptop announcing a new email had arrived for him. He went inside to see who it was. The heading read, "Are you safe? A. L." Ana was trying to contact him as he hoped she would. He clicked on the icon and read the message. "I hope you're ok. I managed to elude them and am in a safe place. I want to see you. Let me know where you are; I'll come to you. Ana." Rafael had gone out to see his sister and get some groceries and wouldn't be back for some time. Rafael will be surprised to see Ana, he thought. It would be safe to send her the address. He typed in Rafael's address on Logan Avenue and indicated that she should punch in 118 on the keyboard at the entrance; "I'll let you in." He was elated to have a part of his life back that had some promise. He left his laptop on to receive her email announcing her arrival. After an hour, he went back out on the balcony in the hope of seeing her. There were a few cars parked by the curb in front of the building. Two men got out of a car further up the street and walked to the entrance of Rafael's building. At that same moment an ambulance siren blaring turned sharply at the corner at Gowan Avenue and parked in front of the building with all warning lights blinking. Two men in white medical jackets pulled a gurney from the back and placed oxygen tanks on their backs. They entered the building. Manuel assumed that someone must need CPR. He went back to his computer and made notes concerning the novel he decided to write.

Memory is unreliable and can never complete the authentic truth of past events. Memoir insists that the author owns his truth.

Fiction distances me from my father's lived experiences. What are the lines between truth and fiction, literature, and life?

The self is an archive that can supply effective forms of testimony. Make it less about remembering events and more about creating and giving meaning to them.

Be less concerned with recovering historical fact. Use fiction to give new symbolic and emotional meaning.

How can I write about the Genocide at my age, over a hundred and seven years after the events?

Can make the self out of real experiences, fiction, and fantasies.

Then a sudden, loud, and aggressive series of knocks pounded the door.

"Ambulance! Emergency Medical Technician! Open the door! Hurry!"

Having seen them from the balcony moments earlier, Manuel thought this was very odd. How could they mistake the apartment? There was a clicking at the door just before they stormed in, bowling Manuel over, causing him to hit his head hard on the floor. The tall one quickly closed the door behind them. The smaller of the two placed a plastic mask over Manuel's nose and turned on the tank that was on his back. Manuel in shock and feeling groggy looked up and saw only blurred faces over him. He began to feel less pain as the sound and images began to disappear. There was a hissing noise as he felt himself falling into a deep hole. Then he was surfing the air on a hard board. The last thing he heard was the smaller one saying, "Yeah, he's out."

14

Manuel wanted to open his eyes, but his head ached when he tried. He attempted a slow turn to his side, but the sharp pain in his neck prevented him. He put his hands on his head and whispered, "What happened? What have they done to me?" He opened his eyes and saw in the dull yellow light that he was in a small concrete room. There was a stainless-steel sink and toilet against the wall opposite him and a table and two chairs near the door to his right. He forced himself to sit up through the pain and dizziness. Turning slowly, he saw that the door had a small window in it. Still feeling dizzy, he maneuvered himself so that he was leaning against the wall next to which the bed was placed. He bumped back against the wall and took a deep breath. He was sore everywhere, his back and neck in particular. A voice without a body emanated from the ceiling, telling him that he had a very mild concussion and that there was a bottle of water and medication on the table and that he should take it. He rose and walked unsteadily to the table and drained the bottle then put it down and flushed the pills down the toilet. "There was no need to break into my friend's place and harm me. If you had asked me to have an interview, I would have come in with my lawyer." There was silence. In a controlled tone, he asked, "Who are you and where am I?"

"You might guess," said the voice.

"Paris, July 15, 1983. *Orly, n'est-ce pas?*"

"Of course. You remember."

"I was in Paris, at the Bibliothèque Nationale."

"Researching Céline. How appropriate."

"If you know all that, you must know that I wasn't at Orly Airport. I didn't participate in the attack."

"We will have time to go over all that. Time to talk about your father. First you need time to heal from your unfortunate passage here. It must have been quite a shock. Perhaps you expected you would end up here. It won't take too long to get used to all this. Food will be served shortly. For dessert tonight there is pastry with an apricot filling and a cup of espresso. Just as mommy used to make. Just as you had in that café in Kensington Market."

"Tell me what you want."

"The truth."

"As if you would know."

"You must be tired and bored. Tell me what book you would like to read. It will be on the table with supper. We want to keep your mind stimulated."

"The only appropriate book under the circumstance is *The Trial*."

"Kafka, how predictable. But there won't be a trial."

"There is always a trial for people like you."

"A confession will end all this. Then you can return to your pathetic life of being a hack writer, sitting day after day in the library you and your father had amassed as a wall to prevent you from integrating into the world."

"Confess that for years you knew the truth about the Genocide but chose to protect the murderers. Commercial ties with the perpetrators were more important."

"Governments change. Apparently, you haven't. It is clear to us that you are guilty. You will confess. It will be easier on you. Enjoy your supper."

"Where's my friend?"

"We left a note for him from the fire department that there was a gas leak we had to check, also that all repairs to the door will be covered. We wrote that you left and would contact him later and that he shouldn't worry."

"Very considerate of you. What did you do with my manuscript?"

"It's here along with your laptop. You'll have the manuscript tonight. We're anxious to see how it ends. Our tech team is going through your computer. You should rest. We'll continue our discussion later."

With time, he began to feel better. The physical pain disappeared. His life took on a dull routine that proved to be more painful, like an abscessed tooth. Three square meals a day under a dull yellow light as well as small cups of espresso, they had done their research, water, followed by fruit and pastry. He began to wonder if they were buttering him up for another assault. He hadn't heard the voice of big brother for some time. It didn't take long to lose the notion of hours and days. He had no idea how many had passed? They piped in fresh air which helped him forget. It was likely spiked, he thought. Occasionally, he found himself whistling or singing along to the repetitive, mind-numbing tunes they bombarded him with. Finally, his head had stopped aching, and he could see clearly. His constitution was strong. He did all he could to avoid raising his stress level. Giving in to his fate, would soon lead to him cratering. Never, he said over and over again in his mind. To pass the time and to keep a record of his illegal capture and incarceration, Manuel focused on writing the narrative of the events in a notebook that was left on the table along with a pencil. Randomly, he took to shouting, "What about due process? I want to see my lawyer." His captor remained silent.

He couldn't even trust his natural sleeping cycles to give him an idea of days and nights. He exercised and wrote to fight off lethargy. It was his way of putting a note in a bottle and throwing it into the ocean in the hope that someone would find it. After having written a hundred and forty pages, the burning need for someone to find him, for the world to know that he was alive and being held captive by an out-of-control element of his government began to wear him down. Sleep. Exercise. Eat. Write. It's very much like my life before, he thought, except now I have no freedom to do other things if I want to. I don't think anyone knows that I'm missing. Or cares. Except Aaron and Ana. Maybe they're just down the hall.

Having researched and written about many writers such as William Saroyan, Dashiell Hammett, Raymond Chandler, Albert Camus, David Goodis, and Philip Kerr over the years when he was a professor, Manuel knew that it was possible to see the internalized and evolving story of the self that a person constructs to make sense and meaning out of his or her life. Not only is this a reconstruction of the autobiographical past, but it is also a narrative anticipation of an imagined future that can help explain the person. Manuel knew that he had slipped back into his academic persona as a layer of protection. He smiled and told himself to blame it on years of training and the pleasure and enjoyment in using language to explore the precision and complexity of ideas. He knew that by taking the disparate elements of a life and putting them together in a narrative, one can discover a more coherent account of identity over time and get a stronger sense of unity and purpose and meaning. The result is a deeper understanding of a life. Even mine, he thought.

He was certain that his inquisitor had done this on his life and believed he had found Manuel's writing full of contamination stories of lives gone from good to bad. However, if he has read my work carefully, he thought, he will have found them to be stories of redemption, about lives that transition from bad to good through action. Raising his head toward the ceiling, Manuel spoke, "Inquisitor, when you read this, ask yourself what stories do. Certainly, they entertain and deal with human emotions as I'm sure you have discovered if you've read anything beyond reports and government docs. They also provide lessons on virtue and morality. Perhaps you skipped over these sections. In a society that has suffered genocide, stories can detail the importance of human experience and interaction. They can heal broken bonds after trauma. At their very best, stories can teach us how to be human."

Despite the silence, Manuel continued. "When you read my writing you will discover my story, my narrative identity, the story of how I am the person I am becoming even at my age. Perhaps for the first time, I have realized that the narrative of identity I have created is the result of self and community. My father would be delighted to hear this. He was always effusive with me. And critical. When he made a strong point in a discussion, he would stare pointedly at me. He loved to engage with people. He must have thought that his son was too inward. I don't think he ever believed that I understood that he tried to integrate the trauma he lived with all his life with his self by narrating it to others. Representing his trauma symbolically in written form enabled this integration. Performing the unconscious, acting out, was his way of working through and complementing his testimonial texts. I know now that I was too wrapped up in my own work and being to the point that I didn't see that he wanted me to be his empathetic witness to accompany him and enable working through his process. He needed me to be an emotional co-presence, a secondary witness to help him mourn and heal. Perhaps I didn't want to see. Now, I understand that in order to reconcile himself with the trauma of the Genocide, he needed to go beyond his status as a victim, his victim self, and this was to be accomplished by recreating a distinct identity from his past self. However, I was absent from this process. Yes, I chose to be. My father's writing beyond its ability to lead to healing was also meant to be a warning, a lesson. It was grounded in moral comprehension. In this respect, his act of witnessing, like Primo Levi's was both a social practice and a moral imperative. By accompanying my father, sharing in his mourning, I could have been his secondary witness, a partner in his process. I might have been a co-owner of the traumatic event and helped him initiate healing. I failed my father. I wasn't even an interpreter of his survival. Had I accepted my role as a second-generation witness, I could have helped even in some small way shape the memory of the Genocide and the way future generations might understand it. Not to justify my distance with regard to this, I didn't want to understand myself and my connection to Armenian tradition solely in terms of my parents' genocide experience. My Armenian identity had to be more than that. However, the damage was too great and so widespread. For those of us, sons and daughters of the survivors, we were always looking for connections, some confirmation and relationship, a bond to the place where our parents were born and grew, a place and community before the catastrophe. Something that indicated that we had a long history there that cannot be denied. Against that, I and my family have a short history in Canada that has allowed us time to heal and for some to plan revenge. Forgive me, father."

Sometime later after his meal, he sat back and pondered his situation as a son of genocide survivors living in diaspora. He spoke out loud. "Inquisitor, listen. Our freedom is often compromised by what traps us in the nets of the past. You do not know Simon Critchley. He is a professor of Greek tragedy. Listen, you might appreciate this. He wrote 'tragedy enacts that which snags at our being and pulls us back to a past that we disavow.' You're scratching your head now. He continued that our 'freedom is constantly compromised.' This is the weight of the past that entangles us. One would think that denying the past is warranted if one is to progress. Not so as Critchley wrote. This is the kicker. 'To disavow the past is to be destroyed by it – such is tragedy's instruction.' Tragedy exists because we are filled with rage and overwhelmed with grief due to war and genocide. Is it any wonder then that Armenians appear to be trapped in a cycle of revenge, grief and rage. Our lives are full of ghosts of family members and others we never knew. What differentiates the living from the dead is often blurred with the result that there is a moral ambiguity to our actions and what we live with. What is right always exists on both sides as does what is wrong. Setting off a bomb at a Turkish Airlines counter at Orly is justified as an act of revenge against a government that still denies that the Ottoman government massacred a million and a half Armenians in 1915 until the end of the World War I and that after the war forced many of the remnant community into exile without compensation for the loss of property and commercial interests. At the same time, the killing of innocent lives at the airport is a despicable act. The past is not through with us."

"My father taught me that what will be remembered of the Armenian Genocide will depend in large part on how it is remembered; that is, the texts that give it form: memoirs, oral history, scholarly analysis, political tracts, poetry, fiction, and drama, for example. History never discloses independently from the various ways we have understood it. I have always believed that the imagination has to be engaged in the representation of the truth. All writing is construction; when we write, we construct new versions of the world. Since the early twentieth century, the nature of large-scale traumatic events such as genocide has compelled writers to become witnesses to criminal acts and to adopt more realistic forms of representation; consequently, documentary realism has become the preferred style because it is forceful and convincing. My father's memoirs documented his survival and are a testimony to his life after the Genocide. His life was an admirable exemplum and was the legacy he bequeathed me. I refused it. How could have I accepted its demands without denying the freedom to explore my own future? If only he could see where I have ended up. He would tighten his lips and skewer me with his piercing look and say, 'You see, my son, it never ends.'"

Manuel got up and went to the table and opened a new bottle of water and drank. "Inquisitor, I've often wondered about the intergenerational transmission of trauma. How our ancestors' trauma is passed down, an emotional inheritance, if you will, not only for my generation, but also as a trace in future generations? The secrets we carry inside us contain those of our personal life experiences but also those we unknowingly bear such as the memories, feelings, and trauma we have inherited from former generations. I don't know how much I would want my children to have this on them. In any case, it's too late for me. I have no offspring. I can hear my father chiding me from the grave. It ends with me. Still, something was required. Something had to be done to remind the world that there is a cost to pay for mass murder."

A long silence passed. Manuel was certain he could hear the Inquisitor breathing, his lungs crackling through the airwaves, through the concrete. A reminder he was human if only slightly.

"You are thinking that I did something to remind the world of the unpunished Genocide. The pitiless voice of the inquisitor wants me to confess. He believes that it will lead to rehabilitation. In fact, he believes that my confession will lead to my being punished which after a certain amount of time will then allow him to grant me absolution, followed by rehabilitation and finally reintegration. Father Confessor must be smugly satisfied in his private confessional. He wants me to say, 'I did it.' He needs my confession of guilt in order to affirm his ritual and thereby maintain his confessional machine. You cannot convince me that I will be free only when I submit to you and hand over my freedom to you. I refuse your sacrament. Go to hell!"

Manuel lay on his bed and closed his eyes. The many ideas his father had left him filled his mind. One such idea he had developed in a paper he had written in 1975 titled, "Western Armenia as a Palimpsest," had always intrigued him because of its perceptiveness. A palimpsest is a writing surface such as a parchment on which the original text has been partially erased then overwritten by another, thus becoming a multi-layered record. With the passage of time, traces of the original record can reappear. A palimpsest then can preserve the original nature of a text or an image, while at the same time revealing the contamination of one by the other. His father had enlarged the meaning of *text* to mean a country, landscape, city, town or village, an area. It was a key notion that he had developed that also referred to all his projects and accomplishments as well as those of his son. Accordingly, his father's original texts in the diaspora had been overwritten and erased by Manuel's. His father had foreseen it and understood it. It was a process that maintained the uniqueness of his work while exposing the contamination of one by the other. Manuel realized that there was the need to efface his father's by adding to it. It amazed him to realize that certain utterances from his father's writing re-emerged in his own without his being conscious of it. The entanglement and interruption of life in the diaspora was made manifest in the collision of their texts. He sat back hard against the cement wall. His texts had been haunted by his father's. All his attempts to forge a new, separate identity and future had been undermined. The past is never past. For many of his generation, what had been passed down to them was traumatizing because it was so emotionally charged yet at times marked by a lack of details, leading to an elusiveness in some Genocide testimonies. "We walked barefoot past village after village. We were starving but no one gave us food or water. We were pushed on until many just dropped." What was passed down to the sons and daughters of the survivors after the

Genocide was great sadness that needed to be mourned. For some, it spawned great anger that needed to be avenged. Manuel understood that it was not just the traumatic memory that was passed on to his generation that was disturbing, but the way his parents were haunted by it. Their loss and the way it affected their lives in turn haunted Manuel. It never ends.

15

Time had turned into concrete, entrapping and inert. Manuel had become suspended, a specimen from another age caught in amber, easy to classify and keep in its transparent casing. How long would they leave him in this state? He called out every day, but never received a response. He had food and drink and made use of being left alone, undisturbed. He had almost completed the first draft of his new novel. I hope the Inquisitor likes it; he smiled at the thought. Maybe he can write the introduction.

After another chunk of time and yet another read through, he decided to relax and let his mind wander outside the enclosure.

Ana had taken his arm and guided him to *Smyrna* for dinner. After a conversation with Tasso, they sat and ordered. It was a meal his mother would have prepared, bringing tears to his eyes. When they finished, Ana suggested they walk along Danforth. It was a beautiful Toronto summer evening, twenty-five degrees Celsius under a clear but darkening sky. They stopped at various stores and restaurants, looking at the many different menus posted out front then went shopping at food stalls for fresh fruit to take back to her place, then a Greek bakery and finally to a bookstore, which made Manuel edgy. Back on the sidewalk, she kissed him and thanked him for the meal. "It will soon be over," she said and guided him through the throng. At Logan Square, a band was playing Greek music and couples were dancing enthusiastically. In a flash, he thought he saw Rafael washing down a *loukoumades* with a Greek coffee in front of Alexander's café. Manuel stopped and put his hand on Ana's shoulder. "What do you mean, 'It will soon be over'?" She smiled and led him through the crowd. In the jostling, they became separated. He looked around but couldn't find her as the people listening to the music and dancing held him in a rhythmic human circle. He called her name. No reply came. In desperation, he called her name again and woke from his reverie, facing the cement wall. He rose and walked around. "Just another day in my coffin."

Sometime later, he heard, "Are you awake?"

Manuel sat up and stretched as his joints were quite stiff from the hard surface of his bed. "You can see that I am."

"Do you know Kourken Malkhasian?"

When Manuel didn't answer, the Inquisitor repeated his question. "Do you know Kourken Malkhasian?"

He waited a moment before answering, "Never heard of him."

"Are you sure?"

"I think I would have remembered. Who is he, and what is his connection to me being kept in here against my will without any legal proceedings?"

The faint odour of a perfume his mother use to wear suddenly wafted through his cell. He breathed it in and for a moment was transfixed. *Lily of the Valley*. Suddenly, he was a young boy in his parents' bedroom, watching his mother gently dabbing some behind her ears then caressing her chest with it.

"What sorcery is this?"

"Nothing but the power of the mind seeking release."

Manuel gathered himself, "You're setting me up for something. And Malkhasian?"

"A gentleman from the old country. A vague acquaintance of your father."

"He never mentioned him to me."

"Yet he exists. He is the former director of the National Library of the republic he so cherished."

"I see. He's come to claim my father's library and papers. He wants to repatriate his diaspora life to a place he had never been." How does this matter to me so many years after my father's passing?"

"Just this. I am content to leave you here in your new home as a co-conspirator in the bombing at Orly Airport in 1983."

"I never was."

"Yes, I know. We need a confession. People's minds have to be put at rest. They need to know their security services are alert and keeping them safe. Now this is the part you will enjoy. In 1985, your father wrote a paper in which he confessed to aiding and abetting those involved in the execution of the attack."

Manuel shook his head in disbelief. "No. It can't be true."

"He wrote that despite the fact that you were in Paris at the time of the event, you were not involved in any way. You were researching Louis Ferdinand Céline. From our own investigation, we have concluded this to be true."

"I don't believe this. My father would never have done this."

"He left his confession with his friend and colleague, Baruch Curiel, who, as we have discovered, recently passed it on to you. It is now in our possession."

"I don't believe it."

"Have you read it?"

Manuel shook his head.

"Well, believe this then. Your lawyer friend, Aaron, along with your remarkable researcher friend, Ana, have been working hard in the background to get you released. It seems that your father went as far as to engage Kourken Malkhasian to offer you a way out in case you found yourself in trouble. As it stands, the republic is willing to offer you asylum and eventually citizenship if you leave Canada within the week. We have no objection. As it stands, given the new information, we have no grounds to hold you. You are free to go either to the republic or back to your home in the city."

Manuel sat on his cement bed and contemplated this turn of events. His father was such an ardent defender of his homeland. All this time, he was looking after his son, the only other living member of his family. His father's voice came to him during an argument they had years earlier. "My son, there is something you will never know. You never stop being a parent. Wherever you go and whatever you do, you will always remain in some way Armenian."

Ana had brought him a change of clothes from his place and waited for him with Aaron in front of his house. At 12:17, a plain, black Chevy sedan pulled up in front of his home. Manuel opened the door and stepped out. His friends came over to him and hugged him.

Aaron asked, "Do we pack your bags for a long trip?"

"Or…" Ana asked, "do we go into your home and read the draft of your new novella and plan the next steps?"

Manuel looked at his friends and hugged them again. "First things first," he said. He looked at Ana and said, "Call Tasso and tell him to prepare a special meal for three. We have a lot to talk about."

16

After a long and tiring climb, Manuel reached the top floor on which Beach Press had its offices. He walked over to the receptionist's desk and introduced himself to Chaya. "My name is Manuel Sweet. I have a 10:30 appointment with Jane Hayman. She checked her agenda then buzzed the publisher on the intercom. "Your 10:30, Mr. Sweet, has arrived." A crisp reply followed. "Thank you, Chaya. Send him in." Manuel stood for a tense few seconds before entering as he pondered the moment and how it would affect his writing career. He took a deep breath then opened the door and went in.

Jane Hayman was sitting behind a large desk with neat piles of folders beside her. She was writing notes with a Mont Blanc 149 fountain pen and looked up.. "Come in, Manuel. Just give me a second to finish this." She signed her name at the bottom and dated it then lifted her head. "I'm Jane Hayman." She held out her hand. "Very nice to meet you. Please sit down." No doubt you're wondering how we felt about *It Never Ends*. It's a great title, by the way. Our editorial department was almost unanimous in its praise. Two of the three liked the story. One wasn't convinced. I read it and liked it a lot. It has mystery and suspense as a good political thriller should have, and it's a Canadian story that hasn't been told yet. All this means that Beach Press is going to publish your story."

A smile drew itself across Manuel's face. "I'm so happy to hear this."

"We're going to plan the launch for spring to get the Passover-Easter market. That's still months away; we have time to put things in place such as creating the cover, setting up the marketing campaign, interviews, etc. What we'll need from you is a blurb covering the characters, action, and the implications. Include a short history of the Armenian Genocide. As well, write a biography, around a page and a half, from which we can take the most salient elements for our ad campaign."

Manuel followed Jane Hayman as she went through the business end of having a book published. Every now and then, he had to remind himself not to get carried away by the fact that this was finally happening to him at his age. He followed closely as she went through each clause of the contract. There was nothing that was going to disrupt the moment. He signed.

When Jane left her office to speak to Chaya, Manuel noticed a manuscript on her desk written by Lori Simantov. Beside it was a letter congratulating him on his new book that Beach Press was going to publish. It was a good day for both of them.

Jane Hayman returned and shook Manuel's hand once again. "Congratulations. Let's hope that this is just the first. That's it for now. Chaya will be in touch to let you know how things are progressing here and what we need from you. Call us any time."

Manuel put his knapsack over his shoulders and said goodbye to Chaya, who gave him her card and began the long and somewhat precarious descent to Queen Street East. When he reached the sidewalk, he took out his phone and called Ana, who answered right away. He explained everything to her. "I knew it, Manuel. I'm so happy for you. I'm going to call Tasso," she said. "Tonight, we celebrate. I'll call Aaron to join us."

As Manuel walked west towards Woodbine, he saw people standing on the sidewalk, looking in the store windows then looking at him. Surely, they're not, he said to himself. He walked further then looked behind him and saw that two of the people he had passed moments ago were following close behind him. He saw his chance when a streetcar was approaching and suddenly darted across the road. He went into a bakery then after five minutes went back out onto the sidewalk. He continued walking west towards Woodbine. He felt uncomfortable and looked behind him. He noticed that one of the men who had been following him had a droopy eyelid and was now standing beside a young woman, looking in the bakery window. "Damn it," he said, "It never ends."

Held Under

1

Jake Armen wanted to live the writer's life, and there was only one city for him that held out that possibility, Paris. After completing his degree in French studies at the University of Toronto in 1971, he got a job in a glass factory off John Street where the work was hard and dangerous. Several times a week, a worker would get a gash, or a deep slice on his body from broken sheets of glass. Some had to be rushed to hospital with heavy bindings of gauze to stem the spurting of blood on the panes and floor. At nights, he stayed in his room at home and wrote about walking along the Seine or drinking at le Café du Dôme in Montparnasse with other unknown writers. He read until well past midnight every night then worked at the factory the following morning. By mid-April he had saved enough for the flight and then some to live for a while until he found a job or sold a manuscript. On May 1, he packed two bags, making sure he included copies of his stories and poems that had been published in newspapers and journals, kissed his mother and father goodbye and took a taxi to the airport. That was a long time ago. Since then, his output has been modest, a few travel pieces, a story in a Parisian paper he had written in French about a rowing club on the Seine, and two poems in *Waves*, a transatlantic literary review. It wasn't much to show after fifty years of the writing life in the city of light. He earned his daily bread working as an editor for various English language newspapers and journals that flourished in Paris. Writers came and went. There was always a need in the writing business for new hopefuls. Three years ago, Dyan and Gatsby, a literary press in New York, had published his novel, *Minor Swing*, based on Django Reinhardt and Stephan Grappelli's lively and evocative Manouche jazz piece of the same name. He believed he had captured the creative spark that illuminated Paris during the late 1930's and then in the post-war years. Five other companies had passed on Jake's manuscript, but he had refused to give up on it. The book had some success in Europe and received a few good reviews in the U. S. and Canada. Jake called it a *minor* success. He had been away from Toronto for a long time, and over the years had become curious about his home city. He hadn't been in touch with anyone since he had left save for the odd exchange of letters with his parents. Still, he was mildly shocked to learn of his parents' passing in a freak car accident near their home. Their lawyer explained the circumstances and sent him a check from the liquidation of their estate. It wasn't much, but it allowed him to eat better for a few months and buy a larger desk where he could work more comfortably on his stories and novel in his cramped room. There was no point of returning so long after their burial, he reasoned. He was sad for a while, but the writing life demanded much of him. It had been so long now that he could barely remember his father and mother or recall the sound of their voices. Toronto like his parents had become strangers. When he moved away, he had no expectation of ever returning. He knew from the media that there had been so many changes in the city, and he often had the feeling that he should go to see for himself. He rarely thought of the friends he had grown up with. Sitting with them at the Todmorden House or at the pubs around the campus, going over old times, reminiscing about the pranks they had pulled and trouble they had gotten into, classmates, dates, and teachers and profs while sipping foamy beer didn't really appeal to him. His experiences would astonish them, sound strange and other worldly. Despite this, he was feeling homesick after all the years. Lately, he had not been sleeping well; he had felt overwhelmed by loneliness and headaches. He didn't want to admit that he was depressed after so many years in Paris. He had become a local in his quarter. Occasionally, shopkeepers recognized him with a wave. It was nostalgia, he said, a combination of the Greek root, *nostos*, homecoming, and *algos*, sorrow and despair. He fought the feeling. He sat at his new desk and worked even harder on a new story until overcome; he vowed to return if only to rid himself of this aching emptiness. He would become the *nosto*, one who returns home after a great adventure. For the ancient Greeks it was considered heroic for one to return home. In his telling, he would intimate having been metaphorically shipwrecked in a strange place and having suffered trials that tested his metal. His return would elevate his stature upon his arrival. He knew, however, that there were no good old days for him to remember. The sooner he left home, the better he had said; however, his return was an uncertain prospect. The moment presented itself when his American publisher in New York, Dyan and Gatsby, wanted to discuss the prospect of his new novel based on the manuscript he had sent them five months earlier. This was the curse of the writing life – waiting. A short email stated that they were interested in his novel and asked him to come for a meeting. He didn't have much money saved but couldn't miss the chance. He sold off most of the books he had collected over the years and a Selmer-Maccaferri Gypsy jazz guitar that held its value as well as a few other items. He managed to gather enough funds by accepting to take on the translation of a third-rate French novel by a small press in the city. A few days before leaving Paris, Gabe Dyan sent him a message, "Call me when you arrive, Jake. We'll meet that afternoon."

The meeting at their office at 817 Broadway across from the Strand Bookstore proved to be positive. The manuscript he had sent had been passed around the editorial staff. They had questions that were ironed out to everyone's satisfaction. The next day, Reuben Gatsby asked Jake to come in to sign a contract. It all happened quickly and was so unusual that Jake began to have doubts it was real. When Gatsby gave him a small signing bonus, it all became real. He shook hands with his publishers. Dyan told him, "Send us chapters as soon as you can so we can get a flavour of the novel and how it develops after the edits."

Before long, Jake was back on a plane with cash in his wallet and some back-up dollars in his bag, twenty-five minutes away from landing at Pearson International Airport. The new story swirled in his head. He kept hearing Gabe saying, "Send us some chapters as soon as you can." That got his stomach churning. He swallowed a couple of antacid tablets. If he wanted to prolong his career, he had to produce and quickly. There were so many new writers waiting for a chance with a New York publisher. Jake didn't have an agent. He knew they could be a blessing or a curse. Gabe and Reuben were hardnosed as they had to be; the business particularly in New York is very competitive. If a publisher didn't like your work, you likely wouldn't get a second chance. Jake knew there were so many factors affecting the decision to publish a book such as what's popular at the time, trends, reputations, and reading tastes. Jake wrote literary fiction along with a million others hoping for a long career that would pay the bills. Gabe and Reuben really seemed to like his work. Jake grabbed the armrests as the plane suddenly began its descent into Toronto. He began to feel he should have stayed in Paris to work on the new novel. The closer the plane came to landing, the greater the trepidation. He knew his return would dredge up things he didn't want to face. Can one ever really go home?

2

Jake soon realized that renting a car at the airport and driving east on the 401 to the Don Valley Parkway was a big mistake especially in the late afternoon. So much had changed since he had last driven on the highway in his early twenties. There were too many cars and trucks going too fast on too many lanes. It was dizzying. When he exited the parkway onto Don Mills Road south then finally joined the line of cars doing a slow climb up to O'Connor Drive, the streets and the houses came back to him. The familiar was comforting. His pulse quickly returned to normal. He turned right. Everything was recognizable. He drove all the way down to the ninety-degree left turn where Broadview Avenue began. A block later, he was on Don Valley Drive and stopped the car in front of number 45. He was home. Except when he looked at the house, it wasn't as he remembered. The new owner had torn down their home and had built an ugly bunker in its place. It was a great disappointment. He could no longer find the reality of his memories. He wanted to go to the backyard and see if the terraces and rock gardens his father and uncle had dug on the slope of the ravine behind the house were still there. He didn't want to ruin the previous memories. He got out of the car and looked over the Don Valley that stretched out before him all the way to Leaside. It didn't look the same either. He had forgotten that the noisy Parkway now ran through it, and the river along which he had played as a young boy had been rerouted from the bottom of the valley below his home to the other side of the Parkway, and its dark, green water was now controlled by a dam. He walked a few yards towards the end of the street and pushed some branches aside and found that the path he had worn in years ago through numerous descents was still visible. It still called to him. Instinctively, he ducked under the branches and brushed by bunches of dark red choke cherries and began sliding down the steep slope. He grabbed at roots and trees to slow his descent until he came to an unstable stop at the bottom of the first tier. There beside him lay a dead racoon being consumed by a buzzing mass of insects. The second tier farther down, he recalled, led down to the sand cliffs and shale ledges above the rapids in the old course of the river. He moved to his left, looking for the footpath that led to his friend Jimmy Wright's at the end of the street. It had grown over and was impossible to move through. With difficulty, he pulled himself back up to the top and cleaned himself up beside the car. The memories clashed with the reality. He walked to the dead end where his friend, Jimmy, used to live. The three houses that used to be there had disappeared and had been replaced by stone barricade with an aluminum railing. On the other side, where there was once a gentle grassy slope where horses from Freeland's farm off Pottery Road and Hughes's stable next door to Jimmy's grazed; where he and Jimmy used to play had been plowed away to become a very steep grassy incline ending abruptly at the noisy Parkway. It was too dangerous to try to go down to the river that way, but he recalled another way down a few yards to the right where the new steep grass-covered hill ended and the old tree line began. He held tight and dropped several yards then bumped into trees and grabbed other branches as gravity pulled him down, sliding and holding then releasing then finally running out of control onto a paved path made for citizens to enjoy a walk in the valley. He stopped out of breath and touched his left knee that now burned with pain. As he looked around, he realized he was twenty yards from the place where in 1952 Seymour Krantz had drowned. That event had troubled him ever since. He had held it under, kept it inside and refused to confront it. He knew this was one reason for his return.

3

The knot tightened and nausea heaved in his stomach. For a moment, he couldn't feel the ground. Everything seemed to swirl around the riverbank and the lazy flow of the river. The trees melted into one giant chaos of green and brown. He took deep breaths and finally grounded himself and was able to pull himself back up the slope to the street where he slid in behind the wheel of his rental. He released the catch that held the seat upright and fell back with his eyes closed. He continued to take deliberate breaths. Seymour Krantz. The thought of what had happened to him all those years ago had caught up with him; in truth, that day in September 1952 had never really left him. It had followed him to Paris and now all the way back. He wanted to head back to the airport and fly back home. Best to follow through and face it, he knew. To what end he asked himself.

He raised the car seat and drove to Beechwood Crescent, where he had rented a room at a bed and breakfast only five minutes away from his old home. It wasn't the homecoming he had planned after being far away across the ocean for so many years. It was the return he knew would be his, filled with sorrow and despair. Night had begun to fall.

The owner of the bed and breakfast, a woman Jake's age, tall and slender, with long, grey hair pulled back in a ponytail, met him in the foyer and showed him around. "You'll be the only guest. I'm going to close down the season early." She extended her hand, "My name is Janet. My room is downstairs. If you need anything, call me. I'll serve breakfast whenever you like. I can make eggs, pancakes with fresh fruit and yogurt, bacon, sausages, toast, whatever you like. Coffee, of course."

"Thank you, Janet. Coffee, fruit and yogurt with toast will be fine, let's say around 9. I'll probably sleep in as I'm quite tired."

"No problem. I've left the key on the kitchen table.."

She turned and was about to go back down to her room, when she stopped and said, "You look familiar. Did you go to William Burgess and East

York Collegiate? I think we might have been in the same classes."

"You know, I was thinking the same thing. I graduated from William Burgess in 1956 and the high school in '64."

"Yeah, me too," she said. I had Miss Underhill in grade two."

"What a coincidence."

"Go figure. I'm Janet Gordon. Welcome home, Jake. I remember you. You sat at the front by the windows. You've changed, but I can still see you from back then."

"Well, well, Janet Gordon. I remember you too. I think we followed each other all the way through up to grade thirteen."

"You're right. I got a job after at *The Star*. Worked thirty-five years as a crime reporter. You?"

"Who would have guessed? I recall that you were good in English. I finished an Honour BA in French studies then moved to Paris where I've been living ever since. I'm a writer."

"Now it's my turn. Who would have guessed? You were the quiet type. Have you had any success?"

"Some. Minor. I just signed a contract with my New York publisher for a new novel."

"Wow. Congratulations, Jake."

"I'm a little tired right now, but if you don't mind, I'd like to find out what happened to one of our classmates, maybe over breakfast tomorrow."

"Sure. Don't know how much I can help you. When I started work, I left the high school world of teenage angst and was thrown into the world of major crime in Toronto. Staying sane and in a few cases staying alive and getting the story were my priorities. We'll talk tomorrow."

"Thank you, Janet." Jake went to the bedroom and unpacked then fell onto the bed. He looked at the white ceiling and muttered, "Well, well. Janet Gordon. Welcome home indeed." As his mind began to shut down from fatigue, he recalled that he used to have a thing for Janet Gordon in grade twelve. I wonder if she remembers, he thought as he drifted off.

4

Jake slept like a log. He got up at 8:45 and showered then dressed. Upstairs, he saw that Janet had begun to make breakfast. He stepped out onto the verandah and felt the early September morning. The air was still sweet, and the sun's warmth blanketed everything. It was during the second week of school on a day very much like today that Seymour Krantz drowned.

Jake went into the living room and turned on the television and found a news channel broadcasting Toronto news. He sat back and tried to follow, but nothing made sense. Even if some of the issues were the same, the weather, taxes, pollution, traffic, inflation, crime, and local politics, they weren't handled the same way as they were back home. He turned off the television and saw Janet as she came into the kitchen. "I'll put some coffee on," she said. "I hope you slept well. I see you didn't like our news?"

"It's a little disorienting, that's all."

"Scrambled eggs all right? Toast and strawberries? Coffee won't be long."

They sat across from each other at the kitchen table next to the translucent white window curtains and ate. Jake finished and asked for a second cup of coffee. Janet put the dishes and cutlery in the sink. "Okay, Jake, let's reminisce. Who do you want to know about from our school days? I don't recall that you hung out with a group or had a girlfriend."

"True. I was a loner. If I'm being honest, I'm not interested in going over high school days. I always wanted to move on. University then Paris."

"Have you had a good life?"

"So-so. I've done what I've wanted to do. Write. Stories, poems and plays. I make a living…well I get by. I live in a one-room flat in Montparnasse. It has a bed, an armoire, a sink, a hot plate, a desk and a bookshelf. Every time I go out, I have to walk down five flights of stairs, and when I return, it feels like twelve. How about you, Janet? How has your life been?"

"I was devoted to my work at *The Star*. There is always enough crime to keep a gal reporter busy. I was married and got divorced. He wasn't at school with us. I met him at *The Star*. Walter was a reporter from the west end of the city who just didn't understand East York girls. No kids. A few boyfriends over the years and lots of lonely evenings. I opened the B & B three years ago. It helps pay the bills."

"It sounds as if we share the writer's curse. I am interested in finding out more about an event that happened when we were in grade two at William Burgess."

"Seymour Krantz?"

"Yes."

"That was the only one I can remember from that time. It was that moment that motivated me to become a reporter. What do you want to know?"

"I never told anyone this. I lived on Don Valley Drive and played in the valley all the time. The afternoon Seymour drowned, I saw him playing on a log with two older boys, maybe in grade four or five. I stopped to say hi to Seymour. He was climbing on the log that was three quarters in the river. He asked me if I wanted to play. I saw the expression on the older boys' faces, and it wasn't friendly. They were smiling, but I sensed beneath there was something threatening. When Seymour and I were talking, they moved away and turned their backs on us. I couldn't hear what they were saying."

"Are you implying that they pushed Seymour into the river?"

"This has bothered me ever since. I have no proof other than a feeling."

"As I recall, the two older boys said that they tried to save Seymour, but his pants had gotten caught on a broken branch, and when the log rolled over, they couldn't release him. The whole school had a memorial for him."

"I remember. Do you know if I could I have access to the lab and forensic reports?"

"Maybe, but it might be easier for me as I use to deal with Police Services all the time."

"You'll help me then?"

"Yes. I want to know now what really happened to poor Seymour. Give me a day to see what I can find. In the meantime, reacquaint yourself with the neighbourhood."

"I will. Let me take you to Ted's Restaurant tonight. It'll be a weird trip down memory lane. Not sure I'm ready for it."

"It'll be fun. It hasn't really changed in all these years, except Ted is no longer with us."

As Janet turned to go to her room, her hair swung away from her face to reveal a deep scar behind her left ear."

5

Ted's Restaurant hadn't really changed since Jake last sat at a booth with friends sixty-two years ago. The vinyl on the seats had changed to dark brown instead of orange; the twirling stools at the counter were still there now with dark red tops. The old-style milkshake maker still sat on the stainless-steel counter against the wall as did the perpetual carafe of coffee warming on a burner. The six-slice toaster was close to the flattop grill off to the right where three hamburgers were sizzling away, one with a slice of processed orange cheese on top. Instead of neon lights, there was subdued lighting throughout. What hadn't changed in the restaurant were the three booths as one entered on the left next to the large front window. They were prized because those seated there could be seen by everyone entering, and they in turn could comment on everyone as they stepped in. The only things missing were the juke boxes, five cents a play or five for twenty-five cents. The noise from the supper crowd was suppressed to a hum. This was in contrast to the rock and roll fifties. The odour of the food cooking on the grill and in the stove was not unpleasant. Jake was tempted to order chips with gravy and a cherry coke as he did when his mother gave him a quarter for lunch which was plenty in 1953.

Jake chose one of the booths by the front windows and waited for Janet who had told him that she would be along shortly as she was putting some material together that she had found that morning on the death of Seymour Krantz. He ordered a black coffee and took a sip and winced. He pushed the cup aside just as Janet entered and sat on the bench across from him. "Best not to think about the coffee," she said. "I'll make you an espresso later. I found some things about Seymour's case," she said as she pulled a small sheaf of papers from her briefcase. "I know some of the people still at police headquarters. One of them, Mike Farnsworth, whom I interviewed many times on some of the grizzliest cases in the city, took me into the archives and helped me find the box with the material from the investigation. When the police arrived on the scene around 4:48 that afternoon, there were a few people around besides the two older boys. There was Evan Winslow, the man who had stopped and pulled Seymour out, and there was the body of Seymour. There were also four drivers who had stopped when they saw there was a problem. According to the report, two boys were sitting on the riverbank, Tom Wilkinson and Billy Noble. They told the police that they had been playing on the large log with Seymour. Here's the thing. The log was mostly in the river. According to Wilkinson and Noble, the log suddenly moved and slid deeper into the river. The two older boys jumped off, but Seymour lost his balance and fell into the river and didn't come back up. Wilkinson and Noble went in to get him and found that the short pants he was wearing had become snagged on branches. They said they had tried but couldn't get him free. The man who pulled him out, Evan Winslow, said Seymour was lifeless when he laid him on the riverbank. The police officer said that Seymour appeared to be dead when he arrived."

"That's it? That's all there was in the reports."

"Well, there was the autopsy report indicating drowning. The report also found one large cut on his forehead and many smaller ones as well as contusions on his forehead and face, likely occurring when Seymour fell off the log. The conclusion was that he had hit his head on the log and when he was snagged underwater, the movement of the log in the current scraped his head and face against the river bottom."

"Poor kid. Is that all then?"

"Listen to this. The report also points to bruised ribs on the left side of his chest as if he had been hit by something."

"Or maybe punched."

"That's what I was thinking, Jake."

Janet put the papers back in her bag. "I can write this up for you, like I used to do at *The Star*. Make it a crime report column. It took me back, Jake. It's a lot sadder when it's someone you knew."

"That's the truth. Not like fiction."

"I'll put the reports on the kitchen table. You can have them."

They ate fish and chips then walked slowly back to Janet's. "I'm getting a little nostalgic walking in the old neighbourhood. Do you remember *Bill's Fish and Chips* on Pape between Cosburn and Gowan? There was always a long lineup of Catholics on Friday nights."

"My father always brought them home wrapped in newspaper. Are you Catholic, Jake?"

"No, I'm Jewish. We were the only Jewish family in the neighbourhood back then until Seymour's family moved in."

"I had no idea. You were just like the rest of us."

"Still am."

When they arrived at Janet's, she put the reports on the kitchen table. Jake picked them up. "Janet, do you know what happened to the two older boys? Did they graduate from high school or go to university? I wonder how they turned out."

"I could do a search. You're here for two more days. I'll let you know. This is fun, also a little creepy. Goodnight."

Jake lay in bed thinking about Seymour's broken ribs. As he drifted off, Gabe and Reuben came to him. *Send us some chapters. We want to know where the story is going.* Jake had a good idea about the ribs.

6

In the morning, Janet served pancakes with blueberries, yogurt and a drizzle of maple syrup on top for Jake as well as a cup of Americano. "This is a treat," Jake said as he dug into the short stack of flapjacks. "I haven't had these in years. I eat crêpes in Paris."

"It's my way of welcoming you home," Janet said. "I have my morning planned out. I'll find out what I can about Wilkinson and Noble."

"Thank you, that's great." I'm going down Pottery Road to look over the area where Seymour died. Maybe I'll pick up something."

"Okay. It's nine now. Let's meet back here for lunch at twelve-thirty. I'll make sandwiches."

"I'll see you then." Jake put a notebook and pen in his knapsack and checked the charge on his phone and went to his car. He drove without thinking as the route had remained encoded in his memory. He applied the brakes around the sharp curves and followed Pottery Road down to the bottom past the old Whitewood riding stables where his mother would take him on his birthdays for a ride along the river side. He saw in the rearview mirror how steep the road was and smiled as he recalled that one of the tests of manhood for him and his pals growing up was the ability to start at the bottom on their bikes and pedal all the way up to Broadview Avenue without stopping.

In front of him was the Pottery Road bridge with its distinctive cement arches rising high above the Don River. There lay the second test of manhood for the young boys back then. One had to stand tall and climb all the way up and over the arch, which was no more than a foot wide, and walk down the other side back down to the street. Jake smiled as he knew he had earned badges for both these trials.

He turned right into the parking lot at the beginning of the paved, walking trail and backed into a spot so that he was facing the bridge and the river. He didn't get out right away as a rush of emotions hit him, the kid from East York who had left the city and had lived for years, writing in Paris. He never thought he would be revisiting the site where he had spent a good deal of his youth. His home on Don Valley Drive was just behind him up on top of the valley cliffs. He thought of his mother and father and all they had lived through and how in the end he had left them to strike out on his own to make his mark. Yet every time he thought of them, the word *abandoned* filled his mind and left him with regret. He stared straight ahead and saw off to the right not twenty-five yards away the place where Seymour had gone into the water. He felt regret because he had spoken to his classmate perhaps only moments before he went into the river. Jake had abandoned him and carried the guilt of his walking away when he might have been able to save him, taken him back up the hill to his place where his mother would have invited Seymour to stay for supper. They would have spoken the *mama loshen;* things would have been fine when he walked Seymour home.

Jake got out of the car and walked across the bridge. Next to the train tracks there used to be a pond with bullrushes around it. He went over and saw that it was still there. He and Jimmy had built a small raft on which they sunbathed and jumped into the water. They always carried a mason jar in their backpacks in which they put the tadpoles they had captured and took back home. Suddenly, a train horn sounded down the tracks as it sped from the north heading downtown. He remembered that when they had heard the train horn on those bright sunny summer days, they would rush up to the tracks to put pennies on the metal rails for the locomotive to flatten. These would be valuable souvenirs of the slow, hot days spent in the valley.

He turned to go back to the car and found himself facing one of the high cement arches of the bridge. Do I dare? He wondered. He put his right foot at the bottom of the arch then lifted and planted his left foot next to it. He slowly raised his right foot and moved it further up then moved his other foot next to it. Stand tall, he told himself. He repeated this twice more and found himself a quarter of the way up one side of the arch. The angle was too sharp, and as he looked around, he began to lose his balance. Stand tall, he told himself but couldn't as he was about to fall twenty feet into the dark green water below. To save himself he dropped to his knees and held tight as he moved backwards on his knees down to the street. Shaken and trembling, he walked back to the car.

He pulled the door shut and gathered himself as he sat and took deep breaths and muttered, "What the hell was I thinking? I'm seventy-seven." There in front of him was the place where Seymour was playing on the log and where he went in. He asked himself, what am I going to learn by looking at the mud and dirty water seventy years later? It's in the hearts and minds of the two boys that I'll find an answer.

7

When Jake had finished his lunch, he cleared his plate, cutlery and cup off the table and put them on the kitchen counter. Janet heard that he had finished and called to him. "Come into my office, Jake. I have some things to show you." Jake washed and dried his hands and went into Janet's office which consisted of a large, brown desk for her computer and printer and two walls of shelving full of books and papers from her years as a reporter and a row of archive boxes on the floor.

Jake looked around and said, "It's still a working office I see."

"It is. My parents left me their house. It's where I was born and grew up. I've been here ever since. Come and sit down," she said. "I've found some things that will interest you."

"About Seymour?" he asked.

"Not directly," she told him. "But things that might explain Wilkinson and Noble and account for their actions."

"I'm all ears."

"I'll begin by giving you the background and some social history then will get to the two boys."

Jake sat on the chair and took out a notebook and pen then nodded that he was ready.

"Tom Wilkinson was born in 1943 on Waverly Road off Queen Street East in The Beaches. It's called The Beach now. When he was five, his mother divorced Tom's father and moved with her son to Gowan Avenue in East York, which put him in the catchment for William Burgess Public School in 1948. Billy Noble was also born in 1943 and grew up on Lee Avenue in The Beaches. His father died in the war when the boy was only one. Shortly after, his mother moved in with her sister's family on Gamble Avenue, a short distance from here. She never remarried that I could find. Noble and Wilkinson were in the same class at William Burgess, and by the time Seymour Krantz's family had arrived from Europe in 1950, Noble and Wilkinson had become good friends. We know from a restraining order that Mrs. Wilkinson had filed with the police against her ex, complaining that he was a dangerous influence on Tom and that she was worried he was feeding him crazy racist ideas about white superiority and hatred toward Jews, Italians, and blacks in the city. Now, here is where I have to give you some background to the social history of the city in the 1930's, particularly in The Beaches."

"Janet, I have to tell you that when I was twelve, my friends and I would ride our bikes down to The Beaches to swim. It was clear to me that it was a very English part of the city back then. I can recall that on Sundays, the Salvation Army band would hold a concert at Kew Gardens."

"Jake, we were both born and grew up in the city. It has changed a lot. Even before you left. What I discovered in digging into the background was shocking though perhaps not surprising. Have you ever heard of the Swastika Club?"

Jake shook his head.

"I remember the Balmy Beach Canoe Club being a very English Protestant place with its manicured bowling greens. Things changed in 1933. Toronto was beginning to become more diverse. In the early thirties, Jews made up only 7.2 percent of the city's population and were the second largest minority community back then.

Anti-Semitism wasn't uncommon; Jews felt like second-class citizens. Many members of the Jewish community at that time were poor and were from the working class. In the summers, Jewish families would go to The Beaches to swim. You can imagine how the staid, upright citizens of Toronto the good reacted to the numbers of people speaking a foreign language, eating different food, and having different habits on their beaches. Local residents complained of the invasion as they called it, and this gave rise to the Swastika Club in the city which openly displayed the swastika to indicate that Jews were not wanted in their neighbourhood. Remember that on January 30, 1933, Hitler was elected Chancellor of Germany. His influence on anyone with a grievance even in Canada was real then. To reinforce this, a number of young people wore the symbol as they walked along the boardwalk. Tensions between various groups in Toronto were very high.

This culminated during a baseball game at Christie Pits on August 16, 1933, between a predominantly Jewish baseball team including some Italian players from the Harbord Playground playing against St. Peter's which was sponsored by St. Peter's Catholic Church at Bathurst and Bloor. At the end of the second game of a two-game series, the Pit Gang displayed a blanket with a large swastika on it and shouted *Heil Hitler.* Jews in the stands rushed to bring the blanket down and a riot ensued as people from the neighbourhood and elsewhere clashed. In all some 10,000 were involved. Bats, sticks and tools were used; miraculously, no one died although many were injured. That's the context in which Wilkinson and Noble were raised."

"That's incredible, Janet."

"Crazy, isn't it? It was exciting to become a crime reporter again if only for a moment. We can only guess that the boys' fathers might have been involved and passed on their hate for Jews to their sons, particularly Tom Wilkinson's."

"And may have led them to push Seymour in and let him drown."

"Yes. Neither of the boys nor their parents left any written statement. I couldn't find anything on the grandparents."

"So, all we have is speculation. We can't go forward with that."

"The Krantz family has disappeared from the record."

Jake went over to Janet and hugged her. "I felt anger before. Now all I feel is sad. One final question, Janet. Are either of the boys still alive? They were only a couple of years older than us."

"The instincts I developed as a crime reporter over many years are still intact. I discovered that Tom Wilkinson died in a shootout with police during a bank robbery in Scarborough in 1971."

"That's the year I left for France. Anything on Billy Noble?"

"He still lives with his cousin in their house on Gamble Avenue. There are no police records on him. He left school and went to trade school as soon as he could and became a plumber. He never worked for a company but did odd jobs and earned a living that way. His cousin worked at Eaton's for years. She died four years ago."

They looked at each other. A smile crossed their lips. "Should we pay him a visit?" Jake asked.

"Oh, yeah," Janet said as she nodded. "He lives only five minutes from here."

"I wonder if he'll remember us?" Jake asked then added, "I wonder if he remembers Seymour Krantz?"

8

After deciding to pay a visit to Billy Noble, Jake and Janet discussed how they would approach him and how they would broach the subject of Seymour Krantz. What would they do if he remembered him and the incident? What would they say if he claimed he didn't recall it? To clear their minds, they went for a long walk around the neighbourhood. Jake showed Janet where he was born on Don Valley Drive. "That's the site, but it isn't the same house," he said. "It was torn down for this ugly wall of bricks to be built. It's sad, but I still have memories of our family here and the wonderful terraces my father and uncle had built all the way down the ravine in the backyard. Being here makes me wonder why I ever left." They turned and looked across the street over the valley that opened before them. Janet saw that returning had troubled Jake. It wasn't just the death of Seymour. "You did what you felt you had to do at the time, Jake. You needed to escape to put yourself in a new environment to write."

"Perhaps if I had achieved greater success by leaving…," Jake said wistfully and recalled the excitement of descending down into the valley in front of his home. The exhilaration of those moments came alive. "This was my escape back then, Janet. I always saw something new each time I went down, learned something new. I miss it, the freshness, the mystery, the encounter with the new and unknowable. I hate getting old, Janet. There's so much regret and not much to look forward to."

"You have a book contract. That's something. And remember, we're doing this for Seymour."

"Yes, but I'm also doing it for me."

Janet didn't understand but didn't ask what he had meant by this. She took his arm, and they started walking back to her house.

After an early supper at Ted's Restaurant, they returned to Janet's home and sat in the living room, drinking wine and reminiscing about their youth in the city. He was relaxed being with Janet. "You know," he said, "I had a thing for you in grade twelve." She smiled and told him, "I remember. Why didn't you ask me out?" Jake laughed, "I was hoping you were going to ask me to the Sadie Hawkins dance." She looked at him and said, "I wish I had. Who knows how that might have changed things." They continued talking until midnight then decided to turn in. Jake got up and began walking to his room. "Let's hope we're sharp tomorrow," he said. "I really don't know what to expect." Janet put her arms around Jake and kissed him. "I'm glad you returned, Jake."

Janet pulled her car up to the curb across from the house where Billy Noble lived on Gamble Avenue sixty metres down from Donlands Avenue. It was the typical two-story, dark-red, brick home on the street, likely built around 1945, with a small patch of grass out front and cement steps leading up to a veranda. The day had started sunny but now had turned cloudy, and a swirling wind began to blow leaves and debris in angry circles. "It looks dark," Janet said. "I don't see any light inside." They walked up to the front door and stopped. There was no ringer or knocker. Janet formed a fist and knocked firmly. There was no sound from inside. She waited a moment then knocked again. They heard the shuffling of feet slowly moving towards the door. Then a gravelly voice, "Hold on. I'm coming." They heard the metal click of the latch unlock the door which opened slowly. They found themselves staring at an unshaven old man, thin as a rail about five feet five, slightly bent over, bald but for a scruffy ring of long, grey hair that hung down around his ears.

"Are you Billy Noble?" Janet asked.

"Who wants to know?"

"We do, Billy. We were at William Burgess Public School with you. Some of us are trying to organize a reunion for those of us who were there in the fifties. Your name was on a list. We were asked to check to see if we can find people and see if there is any interest. Can we come in and talk for a few minutes?"

"William Burgess. That was a lifetime ago. Okay. I'm Billy Noble. Come in." He walked back into the living room with a noticeable limp in his right leg. "I don't remember much about those school years. Didn't have many friends back then."

Janet and Jake followed Billy into a small living room papered with green and blue flowery wallpaper. Billy sat on a well-used armchair, his guests on an old, blue sofa with broken springs. "We were told that you were friends with Tom Wilkinson. Is that true?"

"Tom! My God! Yes, we were friends back then."

"Are you still friends?" Jake asked.

Billy went silent for a moment. "No, I haven't seen him for years. We parted company well before we went on to high school."

Jake stared at Billy, trying to match him to the kid who was playing on the log with Seymour. Billy looked worse for wear after all these years, working as a plumber. His large meaty hands rested on his lap; his fingers were gnarled from hard work and arthritis.

Billy looked at Jake, "Tell me who you are again."

"Jake Armen. You were two years ahead of me and my friend Janet."

Billy's mind was working to recall Jake's name but couldn't through the pipes, hammering, sawing and soldering he had done over the years. "There was someone," he said, "that I sort of remember. Did you live near the valley?"

"I did. I often played in the valley. As a matter of fact, I remember seeing you playing by the Don River. I was in grade two. You must have been with Tom. I recall there was another boy with you. Funny how the mind works."

"I don't remember that."

Jake snapped his fingers, "Seymour Krantz. That's who it was. He was in our class. Do you remember him, Billy?"

A strange look spread across Billy's face. "Is he going to the reunion?" he asked. I'd like to see him again. I think about him every now and then."

"I don't think so," Janet said. He drowned in the river in 1952."

Billy went silent and looked away.

"Do you know how it happened?" Jake asked.

"No, how could I?"

"You were with him when he drowned. You and Tom," Janet said. "Remember? The police came and spoke to you and Tom."

"Since you were playing with him, do you have an idea how it happened?"

"I don't. You have to go now," Billy said and got up and began walking to the front door. He stared at the floor and said, "I won't be going to any reunion."

Jake couldn't help himself. "Did you and Tom push him into the river?"

"No! That's crazy," Billy said angrily. "Tom was playing with him on the log, not me. I was afraid to climb on it. Tom laughed at me and dared me and Seymour. The kid went. I didn't. I want you to go now." His respiration became quicker. He leaned against the wall in the hallway as his right leg gave way.

Jake knew that this was his moment to speak to Billy. "You knew Seymour was Jewish, didn't you. You didn't like him, so you drowned him."

Janet suddenly turned to Jake, surprised by the sudden aggressive tone.

"No, not me. It was Tom, damn it. Damn him. Tom was crazy about things like that. Got it from his father who grew up in The Beaches in the late twenties. I didn't want to. I didn't care about things like that. Seymour seemed like a nice kid. He was new to the country and wanted to learn things from us."

"And Tom Wilkinson drowned him."

"He punched him in the ribs then pushed him off the log. The kid fell in and didn't come up. I waded out into the river and tried to pull him up, but he was caught on the branches of the tree. Tom stayed on the log while I went over to Pottery Road to stop a car for help."

"Billy, I was there maybe five minutes before Tom pushed Seymour in. Remember. I stopped to say hello. Seymour was in my class. He smiled and said hello to me. I left and went home."

"Tom could be a real bastard. After he did it, things were never the same between us."

"Did you tell the police?" Janet asked.

"Tom was a big kid, a bully. He said he would kill me if I told anybody. He said we have to stick to the story that the kid fell in and drowned. I tried to save him but couldn't bring him up."

Billy lowered his head. Anyway, Tom's dead. He turned out bad and was killed during a bank robbery. No one was really surprised. I hadn't seen him for years. Look how this city is. People from all the world come here to live. I fixed their plumbing. Most of us get along. Tom never got along. It was always Jews, Italians, blacks. Please go now. I don't want to think about this. I don't have long anyhow. My heart is bad."

Janet opened the door, and the two walked back to the car. "That was something," she said.

"I've been carrying that with me all these years. I never thought Billy was too," Jake said. "Why didn't he go to the police?"

"Tom bullied him. He must have been afraid, Jake."

Jake shook his head. "All these years."

They drove back to Janet's place. When they got inside, Janet said she was going to make tea. Jake looked out the patio doors at the sky that had turned dark grey. "I need to clear my head. I'm going to sit on your deck and look at the valley."

"I'll bring the tea out and join you. I think we need chamomile and lavender."

Just as Jake opened the door a thunderclap echoed through the valley, shaking the plates and cups on the shelves in front of Janet. The sky ripped open as the boom rolled and echoed away dropping heavy drops of furious rain on everything.

"We'll have to have the tea inside," Jake said and closed the patio door shut and pushed the latch tight.

They sat in the living room and sipped their tea, each waiting for the other to speak. Janet broke the silence. "There's nothing to be done, Jake. Tom has passed away. Seymour's parents must have passed away. We don't know where his family moved to or if he had other family members."

"We could tell the police. Set the record straight. It might offer some a clearer idea of what it was like back then before and after the war here in the city. Given the craziness happening today, it might be a lesson for parents and their children."

"I'd like to think so, Jake, but I'm not convinced. I was a crime reporter for over thirty years. You can't imagine the things I saw and wrote about. Those kinds of lessons don't take when people are either filled with hate or are desperate. They become irrational and act out; others suffer the consequences."

"It's depressing, but you're probably right. Let me propose this. You've written everything up. Why don't we turn it into an investigative report and hand it in to your old paper? If they print it, the police will likely contact them. This is your profession; you should take the lead. We can add an introduction in which we can explain how we came to the story and felt there was something more in it than just the drowning of a seven-year-old boy in the Don River seventy years ago. We were motivated because Seymour was our classmate. It says something about us all."

Janet thought about it for a moment then asked, "And what about Billy Noble? The police might pin a negligence charge against him."

"You're right, Janet. It's not fair. All of this hangs on his testimony."

"He was bullied into silence after seeing Tom Wilkinson drown Seymour. But why didn't he tell the police what really happened that afternoon by the river after Tom Wilkinson was killed?"

"You saw him. He's old and sick now; I'll bet he was a bowl of jelly back then. No need to raise trouble for him now."

A long silence passed between them. The rain stopped as suddenly as it had begun. Jake got up and went to the patio door and looked out over the valley. He could see clearly all the way over to Leaside. Rain drops ran down the tree trunks and gathered in pools of water that drained in rivulets down into the valley. He turned to Janet and asked, "How would you have handled this when you were working?"

"I would have gotten a sworn statement from Billy Noble then run with the story. And you?" she asked. "What would you do?"

"Fiction is a lot easier. You push words around until they make sense, a satisfying story. Real life is always messier. We need to put the story on the computer, print it off and take it to Billy Noble and ask him to sign it. Then you can take it to your editor."

Real life is also a lot more dangerous. I ruffled some feathers about ten years ago when I wrote a piece on Asian gangs in the city. Someone took a shot at me one night as I was walking to my car. The bullet missed but some stone chipped from the building where it hit next to me and caught me here." She pulled back her hair. "I was lucky. The scar is always a reminder." Janet touched his arm. "Yes, I'll take it to my old editor." She looked at him, "It's nice having you here, Jake. I hope you can stay."

9

When Billy Noble opened the front door, his face contorted as if he had just bitten into a lemon. "Not you again. I've nothing more to say to you."

Janet stepped forward. "Billy, we won't stay long. You told us something very important that clears up a mystery."

"Don't think so," Billy mumbled. "I just remember that I wanted you to leave."

"We will in a second, Billy. Janet is a reporter and wrote a piece on what happened to Seymour Krantz. We would like you to read it and sign a paper saying that what is on the pages is what you told us."

"I don't read much. I get muddled easily. I don't have reading glasses."

"Billy, we can sit down together," Janet said. "I'll read slowly what I have written, and you can tell me if anything needs changing."

Billy was getting frustrated. "What the hell is the point. It was all so long ago. Nobody cares now."

"Not true, Janet said. "We all went to school together. Most of us felt the loss of our classmate, Seymour. It was never really explained to us what had happened. But you know. You have the chance to let us know what happened that day. Knowing will bring closure and peace to many of us. It was an awful shock to us as young kids."

"I'm not convinced."

"I think it will help many understand some of the tensions as we were growing up in our end of the city back then," Jake said, "and how it affected one person we all knew."

Billy Noble was still holding onto the front door, keeping it only slightly open. "And how do you plan to do that?"

"I was a reporter for *The Star* for many years. I wrote about events like this every day. Once you approve the piece we've written, I'll take it to my editor. Not long after, it will appear in the paper. People will appreciate that you've done this. Tom Wilkinson is dead. Nothing more can come to him. You'll be helping people remember Seymour. He was just an innocent kid."

Billy Noble stepped back and opened the front door. "Okay, come in then." He limped over to an old dining room table piled with plates and canned goods. "We can sit here. I'll follow along but read slowly. I don't see too well."

Janet sat beside Billy and read slowly through the two pages she had written. Jake looked around Billy's home. It was a mess of old objects and fading memories. A picture of his late cousin leaned precariously against a cracked, dusty green flower vase. Everything was old and used and appeared to have come to the end of its time.

When Janet finished reading the text that she and Jake had written, she asked Billy Noble if he agreed that it was what had happened as he remembered it. He had cupped his hands around his forehead. "Yes, except for one thing. After Seymour was pushed off the log and into the river, I went to get help on Pottery Road because I couldn't bring him up. I was scared and was crying. Tom didn't do a damn thing to help. In fact, he ran away. When I returned with a man to help, Tom was no longer around. Later when the police arrived, I told them what Tom had told me to say.

Tom told me that the police had gone to his house the next day to speak to him. He told them the same story about Seymour slipping off the log and getting caught on a branch. You should add that. I stayed. The bully coward ran away."

Janet wrote down what Billy had said and told him she would add exactly as he had said it. "To make this authentic, Billy, we need you to sign here that you declare that this is a true representation of what had happened that September in 1952."

Billy took the ballpoint pen that Janet was holding and with a shaking hand slowly scratched his name and the date on the line that Janet had drawn at the bottom of the second page. His head sunk low. Please leave now. I'm tired. I need to rest." He rose and limped to the front door. Janet told him that he had done a good deed. Jake thanked him. They left.

When they arrived back at Janet's, she called the editor at the paper with whom she was still in touch. Three times a year he would call to ask her to write a piece for the paper on a crime issue that was troubling the city. Janet explained the story and the background to it, the poignancy of their young classmate murdered while playing in the Don River near Pottery Road. "It all stems from the thirties, Ed," she said, "and the poor way the city handled racism and anti-Semitism. From the thirties to the fifties right up to today. It's the same story. This might be the paper's opportunity to chime in with perspective, maybe raise the social conscience of our fellow citizens. Sometimes we get too smug here being so multicultural. My piece is 582 words long. Whadyasay, Ed?"

"Email it to me, Janet. It might fit into a series we're planning. I'll get back to you as soon as I've read it. Thanks for the call. Bye."

Janet put her cell phone down and smiled at Jake. "I think he's going to take it."

Jake nodded then looked away.

"What's wrong?"

"This is something that should have been done right after it happened."

"Well, we did it now, Jake, and I feel good about it."

"I do too. Don't get me wrong."

"Tell me what's going on."

"Well, for one thing, I have to get ready for my return to Paris."

"Oh, of course."

"Well, I'm not sure I want to go back."

"Isn't that your home?"

"It's where I've been living for the past fifty years. I'm not sure it's my home now."

Janet took his hand. "Come on, Jake. I'll put on some tea, and we can talk about it while we look over the valley."

10

As Jake drove down O'Connor Drive and followed the ninety-degree turn around to his left where the road became Broadview Avenue, he still felt Janet's warmth as she hugged him and said goodbye. "We did something important together, Jake. I'm really happy you stayed with me. We got to know each other. Please keep in touch. Come back when you can." Late last night, Jake had opened up to her about his return to Toronto. He had told her that when he had first arrived in Paris, he didn't feel any emotional distance over being far from home. The new and unfamiliar environment offered so much promise. He was living a writer's life. But after rejection after rejection by journal editors and book publishers, he began to experience isolation and loneliness. During his first years there, he was always overwhelmed and anxious. Then after several years when he had sold a few stories and articles, his sense of self-worth increased. His headaches disappeared. He found he was able to concentrate and produce more.

Occasionally, he would give in to bouts of nostalgia and even entertained the idea of returning to Toronto. He knew that would be an admission of failure. "So I stuck it out, Janet," he had told her, "living frugally, often not having enough for a decent meal. Living this way without significant social connections deprived me of existential meaning. There were times I wasn't sure what I was going to do. How I might end up. Getting the book contract in New York brought me back from the brink. I'm here because I needed to confront things I had left here. The first thing I did when I arrived was to go to Beth Tzedec Memorial Park on Bathurst Street where my parents are buried. I thanked them for all they had done for me, and I apologized for leaving them. They had told me that I should go. 'You'll never have peace if you don't,' my father said. Well, I went, and I still don't have peace. I've done that now and am free to return to Paris, but I like it here. I'm learning to be familiar with my past and accepting despite all the changes. He hugged Janet and told her, "You've become a good friend. I ...," and left it unsaid.

He turned right and descended Pottery Road and pulled off just before the bridge over the Don River and parked very near the place where Seymour was pushed in. His bags on the back seat reminded him of his seven o'clock flight to Paris. He had spent nights writing the experience he and Janet lived through. And more. He was trying to heal himself, for he had blamed himself for abandoning his classmate. How could he have known about Tom Wilkinson was the way he had always rationalized his actions. Yet Jake had felt something was off when he had said goodbye to Seymour who was playing on the log that afternoon. He had chastised himself for not being attentive, attuned to the moment, to Seymour's need.

Jake opened the door and got out of the car and walked to the edge of the river. He felt the pull of the river where he had played in his youth and in an instant sensed that his feet began sliding in the mud into the river. Before he knew it, he lost his balance and fell forward and under the slow-moving water as is flowed lazily toward the Pottery Road bridge. He righted himself in a panic and stood up. He wanted to curse; he wanted to laugh. He turned and walked out of the river and onto the bank, dripping and smelling like the old river.

Jake pulled open the back door of the car and took out a towel and a change of clothes from his suitcase. When he was dry, he sat behind the wheel of the car. As he looked at the river, he let go of what had been troubling him all these years. He had been tangled in the world of experiences that had led him to blame himself for abandoning his parents when he decided to move to Paris. There was no one to look after them as they aged and needed help. Writing in Paris had always been my dream he had told himself. So how did the dream turn out, Jake, he asked himself. And he had abandoned Seymour, a fellow Jew, to a vicious anti-Semite. In his mind, it was proof of a pattern of negligence, something he had always held under. Coming back to the scene of the crime had forced him to deal with his feelings and face who he truly was.

He fell asleep lulled by the slow flow of the Don River. The tension and fatigue during his stay had drained him. Hours later, through bleary eyes, he looked at this watch. It was nine-thirty pm. He had missed his flight to Paris. During his stay, he had debated whether or not to return. Paris had become familiar, but he never lost the feeling that he was a stranger in the same way he had felt before leaving Toronto. It was clear to him that here or there he was always going to feel like an outsider, always the odd man, an observer, never a participant.

He drove back up Pottery Road to Broadview Avenue. Several minutes later he stopped and got out and knocked on the door. Janet opened and smiled at him. "Welcome home, Jake." She hugged and kissed him. "I'll put on some tea."

Port Cities

On an island in the eastern Mediterranean, four people sit in a waterside café discussing their recent roles in two stories in which they were featured. The writer convoked them here, and now they find themselves waiting and hoping for him to arrive and use them again in another project. "What else are we going to do?" was the unanimous response. Every morning, a supply of food and drinks appears. While they wait for their creator, they discuss, argue and tell each other stories.

TIME: now

PLACE: a small café on a sun-drenched island surrounded by the blue waters of the eastern Mediterranean

CHARACTERS

Manuel Sweet, a writer, 77 years old, has a sore back from his last role.

Ana Lekta, 68 years old, tall, slender and beautiful. She is a researcher, has a photographic memory.

Jake Armen, a writer, 77 years old, has lived in Paris since 1973. Has a book contract with a New York publisher.

Janet Gordon, 77 years old is a retired crime reporter for a Toronto newspaper.

As the curtain rises, MANUEL is carrying a bottle of wine which he takes to the table and sits with his fellow characters.

ANA fills each glass with wine. They drink in silence.

ANA: So here we are.

JANET: Yes but where is he? Should have been here by now.

They drink in silence.

JAKE: He can't be too far away.

MANUEL: Well, I don't trust him.

JANET: His word is no good. I recall the early drafts. Full of promise.

JAKE: Right. Things went one way then another (*snaps his fingers*) like that.

ANA: We adapted. Still, can't complain. Look around. I might go down to the beach and take a dip.

MANUEL: What, like yesterday? That didn't work out. It's not in the cards.

JAKE: Not in the ink you mean.

They all chuckle.

MANUEL: Good one. We could have used a little more humour in our story.

JAKE: It was a little grim in parts.

ANA: Yes, but he pulled it off in the end. Almost a happy ending with a promising future.

JANET: (*She holds up her phone*) Look what I just received.

ANA: Tell us then.

MANUEL: Read it, Janet.

JANET: (*She reads*) Something came up. Can't make it. Will try again tomorrow. Carry on without me until.

JAKE: Great. What the hell are we doing here anyway?

JANET: Lounging by the sea, under the sun on this gorgeous island.

ANA: It could be worse. He might have written a war story set during the Battle of Vimy Ridge, April 9, 1917, at 5:30 am. Mud, blood and guts. Three days later, 3,500 Canadian dead and 7,000 wounded but the battle was won. Now that's grim.

JANET: (*Looking at Ana*) We might have been nurses.

JAKE: And I an officer in his majesty's first Toronto Jewish Hussars.

MANUEL: Not likely. Both of us would have been front-line reporters.

JANET: That's my beat, boys.

ANA: Be grateful for the story we got.

MANUEL: It's the waiting that gets me. After all we did for him.

ANA: R and R on this island is his way…

JAKE: His way?

MANUEL: His way…

JANET: His way of saying…

ANA: Thanks for the memories as he moves on and leaves us to lounge by the blue Med.

JAKE: Under the brilliant sun.

MANUEL: In this empty café.

ANA: Now what do we do besides wait for the guy?

> *A brief silence as each contemplates what to do next.*

MANUEL: I remember that in one draft, he had me in Paris, wandering through the city, going to bookstores and sitting in cafés. I got a couple of good poems out of it. But then after ten pages, I lost concentration.

ANA: You mean he did.

MANUEL: Yes. I get confused sometimes. I was sitting in a café near the entrance. I couldn't afford the sidewalk table price for the same coffee. The woman in her mid-twenties sitting next to me began complaining about the price of coffee, croissants, and everything. Then she suddenly went from food to "les juifs qui contrôlent tout." I began to get nervous. How could someone so young have all this pent-up anger against people she likely didn't even know? I wanted to get up and leave, but he wouldn't let me. He kept me there as a foil for this person to spew venom. I was waiting for him to let me argue with her. It was intolerable.

JANET: Well, did he?

MANUEL: In a second draft, we had a reasonable conversation and walked off together along Boulevard Raspail.

JAKE: Back to her place, no doubt.

MANUEL: *Penses-tu?* I was hoping for that especially after making me sit through her rant. I had begun to imagine walking up many flights of stairs in great anticipation, closer and closer to her expectant room.... No chance. He wouldn't give me the pleasure. He scratched over the page with his fountain pen filled with the washable blue ink we all know he uses, *Radical revision needed.* He put me in a drawer and left me there for months. I'm still waiting to see the light of day on that one.

JANET: He can be a bit of a bastard.

JAKE fills everyone's wine glasses.

ANA: (*She raises her glass.*) Here's to better luck on the next one.

They all clink.

ALL TOGETHER: To the next one.

JANET: This was my first time with him so I don't have much experience to share. In this story, I think I come off as knowledgeable and sympathetic. A helper, really. I get a little forceful near the end when we're questioning the old man, Billy Noble. He gave me some latitude to stretch which I did. Of course, at the end, when Jake returns, I am happy but not effusively so. Yet I feel that our connection is based on mutual feelings and respect. I think he pulled that off.

MANUEL: Maybe he got lucky.

ANA: Maybe he does have talent.

JAKE: We'd all like to think that.

JANET: Otherwise, what would we all be?

MANUEL: A happy accident.

ANA checks her phone and reads the message.

ANA: He's on a late-night flight and hopes to be here around midnight if he makes the connections and catches the last ferry to the island.

JAKE: I'll believe it when I see him. He says a lot but doesn't always come through.

JANET: Thus, we wait. Hoping.

ANA: No sure what we're hoping for. Another plot? A role? A chance to be taken out of the drawer?

MANUEL: What else can we do? We depend on him.

JANET: I want to see how he's going to write us out of this one.

JAKE: Maybe we'll find out tonight.

ANA: We complain, but we really should be honoured.

JANET: How so?

ANA: Well, being written and collected means being valued. We have the possibility of being remembered.

MANUEL: People read to learn about themselves. In some cases, certain books become identified as being significant and become part of our tradition and knowledge.

Jake: Who decides this, professor?

ANA: Readers and the literary machine.

JANET: It sounds a little random to me.

JAKE: And our guy?

MANUEL: Don't hold your breath. He's had some success and good press but very limited.

ANA: Consider his age. Sadly, I believe he's run out of time for anything significant to happen. There's not much chance he's going to write a *magnum opus*, and slimmer odds that whatever he writes will be published. Look at his diaspora background and his inward-looking community.

Jake: I know the odds only too well. Not much chance for a descent review or a stimulating literary debate.

MANUEL: From experience, I can say that his mistake was focusing too much on what happened in 1915. He attended to it well, but after a certain time, he should have moved on. He could have found a new voice and a larger readership.

JAKE: The first question a publisher asks is who will buy this book and how many can we sell?

JANET: So even if the work is really good, he won't take it on.

ANA: All this is to say that our time here is likely coming to an end. We should consider moving on. What say you?

ALL: Agreed.

They all look at each other.

JANET: Now what?

MANUEL: I've got a story for you.

They all gather round to listen.

JAKE: He gave me a limited range to work with: brooding, haunted by something in his past. I want to know why I left home. What did I accomplish in Paris that I couldn't have in Toronto? Yes, it was selfish of me. I abandoned my parents to follow my dream. Writing in Paris. Sounds glorious, doesn't it? I lived in one small room with a small bed, a desk and chair and a sink. The one window looked on to a wall of other windows looking onto mine. Dust and noise. The constant climbing to come back upstairs. Crazy prices. The loneliness. All that for a slim novel titled *Minor Swing* and another one that may come out in a year if at all. To eat, I had to edit other people's lousy expat writing on their Paris experience. It wasn't a very moveable feast.

JANET: Still, it gave you a certain something.

JAKE: Not sure he pulled it off.

JANET: We're together at the end, Jake, and we got some closure for Seymour. That's something.

JAKE: I wanted something more.

ALL: To something more!

They all drink.

ANA: He used me in different circumstances before. The beautiful, exotic woman. Except he made me older in this one and gave me something new, a photographic memory. I played it as more of a blessing rather than a curse.

JAKE: You're lucky.

ANA: Consider where he has put us: a port city where people are on the edge, hoping to leave but can't always do so. And where people are on the edge because they are new arrivals, having no connection to anything. They are stuck here. Sound familiar? In port cities, people come and go, admittedly not always willingly. Not us.

Manuel goes to look at a schedule posted on the wall.

MANUEL: There is a ferry leaving for the mainland today one o'clock. That's in twenty minutes. I'm going to be on it. Are you coming with me?

The three join him to look at the schedule then at each other.

JANET: What if he arrives and doesn't find us here?

ANA: He'll just have to find others to do his bidding. I've had it.

JAKE: I'm going.

JANET: Me too.

MANUEL: Good luck to him. Let's go.

> *They all exit.*

Black

About the Author

Lorne Shirinian is Professor Emeritus of English and Comparative Literature, a poet, a novelist, a playwright, literary scholar, and memoirist. He lives in Toronto with his wife Noémi.

www.ingramcontent.com/pod-product-compliance
Lightning Source LLC
Chambersburg PA
CBHW071129130626
46556CB00014B/2437